Lily
and the
Dragon's
Ghost

by

NP Haley

Copyright © 2021

1st edition

ISBN: 978-0-578-89985-5

Formatting by: Ron Haley

Cover by: Pink Ink Designs

Editing by: Ron Vincent

Library of Congress Cataloging-in-Publication Data 2021

Glossary

Term	Definition
Banlow	Romany (gypsy) slang for "pig"
Biretta	A priest's headgear or hat
Bloke	A common man, not of royalty
Bloomers	Loose undergarment reaching from the waist to the knees
Bravado	Courage
Cattails	A plant that can reach a height of 4 to 9 feet.
Coiffured	Styled hair
Dinlow	Romany slang for "idiot"
Discombobulated	Confused
Emanating	Coming out of
Gander	To look
Gobsmacked	Utterly astonished
Homily	A sermon given by a priest or minister
Mississippi Delta	The area where the Mississippi River merges into the Gulf of Mexico. This delta covers 35,000 square miles within seven states!
Mule-Skinner	The driver of a twenty-mule team
Naw'lins	New Orleans

Privy	An outside toilet
Ragman	A person who collects rags, bones and metals, then sells them.
Shirt-waist	A blouse
Stagecoach "Whip" Whip, etc.).	The driver of a stagecoach (Charlie, Jehu, Brother
Vieux Carré	The French Quarter of New Orleans
Knarr Ship	Norse term for ships that were built for Atlantic voyage.
War Between the States	The United States Civil War (1861-1865)
Yog	Romany slang for "fire"

Index

Prologue

My dear readers,

My name is Lily Quinn. I was born in the village of Caruthersville, Missouri not long after the War Between the States. Caruthersville sits so close to the edge of the mighty Mississippi River, that if the entire village sneezed at the same time, the place would simply slip right off into the river and be swept down into the Gulf of Mexico. I'm thinking that's an exaggeration, but that's what some folks say whenever we get together.

Seeing that I was born a few years after the war ended, I don't have first-hand knowledge of its happenings, but the war is close enough in years that it's still fresh on most folks' minds. My friends Ott, Paul and Tom Pruiett have a big bag of tales told to them by their Pa and uncles who fought in the war. So, even though we're about the same age, I guess they ought to know a bit more than me and my best friend Ophelia. But even if they don't, those boys sure do *act* like they know more about it then we do. Then again, those Pruiett boys act like they know more about *everything* in the whole dang world.

I have black, curly hair and my eyes are the color of fine gold (so said my Pa when he was alive) and I'm at a pretty average height for a 13-year-old. I live with my oldest sister Caitlin, her sheriff husband Andre, (who by the way, is a big pain in the behind for me!), my younger brother Benny, and my wild little sister Tessa on our farm on the outskirts of Caruthersville. The farm belonged to Ma and Pa before they were killed by a woman posing as our Aunt Birdie, and now it belongs to the four of us kids. But that's another story to be told.

My best friend Ophelia lives on another farm not too far from ours with her Ma and Pa. She has white-blonde hair and crystal-blue eyes like her father - who came from Sweden, or so I think. She has long, skinny legs, and when she's scared, she can run like a deer, leaving me way behind breathing in her dust! We have been best of friends since the first day we met, and we always seem to get ourselves involved in these ghost happenings – but we don't aim to! Andre, my irritating brother-in-law, says we are like magnets for trouble. It just comes and jumps right up on us like fleas on a dog.

This tale is about our adventure in Mississippi where we met our first dragon-ghost, if you can believe that. But it's the dog-gone truth.

Respectfully yours,

Lily Quinn

1

What a Ride!

"Yee-haaaa! Hang on tight!" Esabella hollered, a huge smile spread from one ear to the other. The three of them lurched forward and backward, and pitching from side to side.

"What a ride!" she shouted gleefully. "Keep 'em going, Mr. Pat, keep 'em going! I haven't had this much fun in a month of Sundays!"

"HEE-YAAAA!!!" bellowed Mr. Pat, the stagecoach driver. His voice boomed over the sound of thundering hooves as he urged the mules to run faster than they should. The stage jerked and shuddered violently as he snapped his whip. They were flying along the open river-road, hitting - so it seemed - every single rut and ridge in the hard, furrowed earth. Dirt and dust whipped through the cracks in the old, weather-worn, wooden floorboards in large, billowing clouds, covering Esabella's shoes and skirt with the powdery particles of the dark-black, fertile soil from the Mississippi delta country.

Clenching the shoddy armrests with white-knuckled fists, Lily Quinn, Ophelia Knudson and Esabella Bloome hung on for dear life. Esabella's face was wreathed in joy as her eyes flashed and sparkled with exhilaration.

"YEE-HAAA!" she shouted again at the top of her voice, lifting a fist into the air. "Make 'em run, Mr. Pat, make 'em run!" Quickly she grabbed at an armrest to keep herself from slipping right off the bench and onto the pitching floor. Her black traveling skirt was bunched up around her knees, and her pristine-white petticoat was wrapped around her thighs, with only her bloomers overing the calves of her legs. Her backside gradually slipped close to the edge of the bench, so she pressed the toes of her satin-covered shoes firmly against Lily's bench. Her fancy traveling hat, full of black and white feathers, was askew; her neatly coiffured hair was now flying wildly around her head in quite untidy, light-blonde ringlets, making her look like a wild woman. She gave the two girls another ecstatic, wide-eyed look, her ice-blue eyes flashing in glee making Lily laugh out loud.

"I'm taking this durn petticoat off! It's way too hot to bother with it, and we might have to make a run for it!" She then lowered her voice to a whisper and added, "One of these days we will all fly like the birds, I tell ya! Mark my words – we'll fly like birds." She gave Lily a quick grin and a wink, then whipped off her hat, and with a sharp snap of her wrist, flung it out the rumbling stage window. Stumbling about to keep her balance, she stood up, reached inside her waistband, untied her petticoat, and yanked it off through her waistband. Out the window it flew, where it was caught by the handle of the stage door and began to flap violently in the wind.

Lily looked at her and burst out laughing. Lily and her friend Ophelia were wearing britches and a shirt - they didn't have to worry about being uncomfortable.

"WHOA!" A hard jolt from the stage flung Esabella onto the bench, yelling. Catching her balance, she turned to Lily. "It's as hot as Hades in this durn wooden bucket, ain't it, Lily-gal?"

Esabella had called Lily this name as long as Lily could remember. "Who decided that we women had to wear petticoats anyways? Probably some dim-witted *man*, if you ask me," she said, laughing loudly. She looked at Lily and Ophelia with glee. "Life's a hoot, ain't it, gals?"

Lily, laughing, thought about how much she loved being around Esabella. Esabella Bloome was in her late twenties, a young woman who had lost her husband in the War Between the States. After her husband's death, she moved in with her brother Otto and her sister Annabelle, in a beautiful, old home in Vicksburg. She was tall and thin, with white-blond hair and sky-blue eyes. Her skin looked as if it were made of porcelain; her long, thick eyelashes encircled her eyes like beautiful black feathers. She was a distant cousin of some sort to Lily's father - Lily couldn't quite remember the exact relation.

Lily sat and laughed, thinking about how deeply she enjoyed spending time with Esabella, until the sudden thunder of horses' hooves just outside the window interrupted her thoughts. All three of them craned their necks to have a look-see out the window.

"Well, butter my biscuits, if it ain't Charlie Juarez, trying to rob us," Esabella said. "I have an awful dislike for that buzzard-brain. I know durn well he's the one who did away with my sister Annabelle, and I'm gonna get 'em if it's the last thing I do on this green Earth. Iff'en I had me a gun I'd get him right here and now!" Immediately she scrambled away from the window, then leaned over and took another quick peek.

She seemed to be mumbling to herself. "Dag-nab it, that ain't Charlie Juarez, that's Buster T, Tobin and he's after *me*! He ain't wanting to rob us, he wants to kill me, 'cuz I know what they did to Annabelle!"

Her face turned as white as snow as she scurried back to the other end of the bench. With wide-eyed alarm, she looked at Lily, then hunkered down, leaned across the narrow opening between the two benches and whispered, "Get down on the floor, gals! It is exactly who I thought it might be. It's that *creature*, Buster T, Tobin from another world. He won't leave me be! If I don't make it to Vicksburg, you find my brother, Otto B. Söderberg! Maybe he'll tell ya about this creature and why he won't leave me be."

Lily stared open-mouthed at Esabella, wondering why she referred to the man as a creature.

CRACK! The sound of a rifle shot echoed across the Mississippi delta and ricocheted through the stage. It sounded as if a glass window had been violently shattered right beside them. The girls instinctively dove for cover on the lurching floor, but Esabella slumped over onto her bench, her eyes wide open, staring into nothingness. A small spot of blood oozed through the shoulder of her white blouse. Slowly, her eyes started to close.

Lily pushed Ophelia aside and scrambled back up onto the bench, her face white with horror. Stunned, Ophelia looked at Lily, and Lily at Ophelia. Then they looked at Esabella. After a couple seconds, Ophelia began to stammer, "I... I... I've seen a lot of dead people, Lily, and Esabella is- "

Ker-plunk! Ophelia's eyes rolled to the back of her head, and she slumped into Lily's lap in a faint. Staring down at her friend, Lily could not believe her best friend had done it again. As was her habit, Ophelia fainted every time she saw (or thought she saw) a dead body.

"Well good grief, Ophelia!" Lily yelled above the racket of the lumbering stage. "Can't you at least wait until we try to help Esabella before you faint?" Lily gave Ophelia a sharp shake and pushed her up into a sitting position, where she propped her head against the doorframe as best she could as the stage continued bouncing wildly along the trail.

"Ophelia!" Lily yelled as she reached across the space between the two benches trying to prevent Esabella's body from sliding off the bench onto the floor. "Help me, Ophelia! We need to help Esabella! We can't let her slide onto the floor, even if she is dead! That's not respectable!"

THUD. Like a slow-moving slug, Ophelia slid off the bench and hit the jolting floor. She moaned loudly but did not open her eyes. Giving Ophelia a gentle push with her foot, Lily stepped gingerly across the tiny space between the two benches and eased Esabella's head onto her lap - which was a chore, since the stage was continually jerking and jolting.

Looking out the window, Lily saw a scruffy-looking man on horseback with his hat pulled low to hide his face, riding parallel with their window. In wide-eyed horror, she watched him raise his rifle and aim for her.

CRACK! Another loud rifle shot rang out. Terrified, she looked up and saw that the rider had been knocked clean off his horse, tumbling head over heels across the grassy field. His horse immediately sprang forward and caught up with the mule team, then passed them like they were standing still. He vanished down the trail like a runaway train.

Pulling back hard on the mules, Mr. Pat and his co-rider, Mr. Porter Smith, leapt from atop the stage. "Esabella!" Mr. Pat yelled, "Y'all a'right back there?"

Lily stuck her head out the window and told him she didn't think so, just as Mr. Porter whipped the door open and looked inside. "Aw horse-hockey, Pat, I'm thinkin' he's done gone and got Esabella," he said quietly.

Mr. Pat elbowed his way past Mr. Porter, jumped into the stage, stepped over Ophelia's body on the floor then sat across from Esabella.

"Gosh a'mighty, Porter. I'm glad you shot the son-of-gun. Pardon me gals…" Lily caught a glimmer of moisture in Mr. Pat's eyes as he reached over and gently brushed his hand along Esabella's face. He turned and looked down at Ophelia, who was still slumped against the wall awkwardly.

"Her too, Lily?" he asked with a frown.

"No, she just fainted, as usual."

"Well, Porter," Mr. Pat sighed, "let's get on out'ta here. Lily, hold onto Esabella and don't let her slip onto the floor."

With that said, the two men climbed back to their seats and Mr. Pat moved the mules out with a sudden jolt. Lily held Esabella tightly, hoping she was still alive. As the stage lurched forward, Lily sat in silence and thought about her cousin Esabella.

***

Esabella was on her way back to Vicksburg because her sister Annabelle had been mysteriously killed in a cave outside the city. Esabella, and Annabelle's husbands had both died in the War Between the States and neither girl again married, nor did their brother Otto after his wife, Janie, passed away due to the Yellow Fever epidemic in New Orleans fifteen some years back. Annabelle and Esabella's husbands had been twin brothers who perished in the Battle of Chickamauga only two miles apart on the very same day in the very same skirmish without knowing the other brother had perished.

Esabella had been in New Orleans visiting relatives when the news of her sister's death reached her. Shortly thereafter, when the news of Annabelle's death reached further north to Caruthersville, Missouri, Lily's sister Caitlin contacted Esabella and asked her to escort Lily and Ophelia to Vicksburg. The girls had been visiting their brother-in-law's cousin Michel because his wife Paulette had given birth to twin baby girls. Since Paulette had eight other wild boys and the new twins were sickly, she was overwhelmed. Caitlin was sure Paulette could use some help, so after sending Paulette a letter, Caitlin sent Lily and Ophelia down to New Orleans on the train so they could help Paulette for a few weeks. They didn't do much work for Paulette, since they were told that keeping the boys busy would be helpful enough. So, they spent their days running wild through the swamps and keeping track of all those "heathen Beaumont kids", as their father called them. After a couple of weeks, however, Paulette wrote Caitlin to thank her for sending the two girls and to say they could go return home since she didn't need their help any longer.

Thus when Esabella heard of her sister's death, she not only agreed to escort the girls home, but she also insisted the girls stay with her for a month or two in Vicksburg to be with the family during the time of mourning. Caitlin agreed, and Lily and Ophelia were more excited to stay in Vicksburg with Esabella than they had been when they found out they were traveling to New Orleans to stay with Michel and Paulette.

***

Shadows grew heavy along the road as dusk slipped quickly into the thick forest. The sun had set, and the bright, sunny day had rapidly morphed into a dark night; the sounds of night creatures slowly escalated. A coyote's mournful cry echoed eerily along the riverbed, then slowly echoed away into the nearby hills. It sent chills dancing down a person's spine as it rang through the dark southern night. From far across the Mississippi river came the lonesome call of another coyote; as if it was answering the first. A slight chilly breeze crept up from the riverbed and caressed Lily's arms like a living thing. She shivered and reached for a stage blanket. In the darkness, Lily noticed Esabella's wound had stopped bleeding. She stopped and stared. Wounds like this normally bled profusely, since it was so close to the heart. If it stopped it was usually because the person had stopped breathing.

Ophelia's weak, but startling, whisper interrupted Lily's thoughts. "What happened?" she said as she pushed herself up from the floor of the still lurching stage.

"You fainted again," Lily replied, annoyingly, "I sure wish you wouldn't do that when we're in times of calamity. Esabella was alive when you fainted, but I think she might be dead now. I can't feel her breathing."

Ophelia's face instantly turned white again as she looked at Esabella. She squeezed her eyes shut, but managed not to faint again. "Maybe she's only in a deep sleep and will wake up again."

Lily shook her head in disagreement. "I don't think so, Ophelia. Feel her arms. Do they feel cold to you?"

"I'm not feeling her arms, she might be dead! I don't touch dead people."

"Come on, Ophelia."

"No."

"Come on."

"No."

"Please?"

"No, no, no, I'm not going to touch her. It's very bad *juju* to touch a dead person!"

"What? I've never in my life heard that. Whoever told you that is full of malarkey."

"My Granny Toots told me, that's who - and she's right! My Uncle Theodore was touching and rubbing Aunt Beanie's arm when she lay in her coffin, and instantly he fell-over dead right there beside her coffin! They had to have a double funeral for the two of them. And when my uncle Chester pulled my uncle Theodore up from the floor, he fell-over dead! So, what do you say about that?"

"I'd say your uncle Theodore and your aunt Beanie were both over 100 years old! And your Uncle Chester was right there on their shirt-tail, being 98!" Lily whispered sharply. "All three of them had one foot in the grave and the other on a banana peel."

"*Hmpf!*" Ophelia snorted. "I'm *not* going to touch her."

Rolling her eyes to the back of her head, Lily sighed and laid her head against the back of the swaying stagecoach.

"Okay, but she won't hurt you."

Ophelia scrambled up onto the bench and crisscrossed her arms across her chest with a look of defiance. "I don't want to keel over dead!" she hissed.

They rode in silence for a few minutes, then Lily eased Esabella's head up from her lap, stood up and slid a rolled-up stage blanket under her head. Lily then scooted across the opening to sit beside Ophelia.

They sat there in silence, staring at Esabella's body.

After a while, Mr. Pat slowed the stage a bit. The bench began rocking them gently back and forth as the rhythm of the stage rocked gently. The two of them waited eagerly for Esabella to moan, groan or do something. Anything.

Nothing happened. As the sky darkened into a deep grey, Mr. Pat slowed his mules to a walk, and the inside of the stage gathered more shadows. A slight glow flickered through the window as Mr. Porter lit the two stagecoach lanterns hanging on either side of the coach.

Leaning her head against the side of the window, Lily gazed out at the night sky. Dark clouds were moving quickly, blocking out any hope of moonlight. Little by little, Lily's eyes closed and her mind grew fuzzy with slumber.

Just as the first images of Lily's dream began forming, she was thrown back into reality when Ophelia grabbed her arm and gave her a sharp jerk. Staring at her friend with wide-eyed, hazy, surprise, Ophelia put a finger to her mouth signaling Lily to not say a word then slowly rolled her eyes towards Esabella; motioning for Lily to look. Goosebumps crawled on Lily's skin as a chill shot up her spine and grabbed the base of her neck. Without moving her head, Lily darted her eyes to where Esabella lay on the rocking bench.

A greenish-white glow hovered above Esabella's motionless body, moving gently in a circular, swaying motion. It shimmered and shook like the leaves in a storm. As they looked, it began spinning faster and faster. Faster than anything the two girls had ever seen.

To their horror, the glow suddenly slowed and morphed into the shape of Esabella's sister, Annabelle.

Quietly pushing themselves against the back of the rocking bench, they sat spellbound with fearful fascination as the image of Annabelle eased itself into a sitting position on Esabella's shoulder but stared at *them* with a solemn frown. The thing's eyes seemed to penetrate deep into their very souls. Slowly a smile crept across the apparition's face as it continued staring at them with its glaring eyes. Lily felt her heart match the pace of a race horse.

Still shimmering and glistening, the apparition started emitting tiny specks of lights, like fireflies which began floating out the window and vanishing into the velvety black sky.

Then they heard it.

Neither girl could see the specter's mouth move, but they certainly could hear it speaking.

"I'm gonna get that cussed creature," the specter whispered. It had Annabelle Bloome's recognizable deep, raspy voice, but it's mouth never opened to speak! "I'm gonna get him good," it said. With a loud *swoosh*, the apparition whisked out the window and vanished.

Esabella's body began to shiver, and the girls heard her moan in pain. Shocked beyond belief, Lily and Ophelia sat stone-still for a second before leaning in closer and staring in total confusion. Lily reached above her head and grabbed another stage blanket to wrap around Esabella's body.

In a barely audible voice as she shivered Esabella mumbled quietly, "Dang, what in tarnation hit me? A cannonball?"

Neither Lily or Ophelia replied. They sat and stared at her with bugged-out eyes, not for one-minute thinking this could be happening in front of them.

"No..." Lily finally whispered. "It was a man with a rifle."

Esabella moaned a bit, then fell silent. Within a few seconds, she began to snore loudly. The girls felt a sense of relief.

Jumping halfway out the window, Ophelia called to Mr. Pat in a loud, unsteady voice, "She's alive!"

Instantly the mules were pulled to a stop and both men jumped from the driver's seat. Wrenching the door open, Mr. Pat jumped inside.

"Butter Bean," he whispered softly, "ya doin' okay, considerin' ya been shot?"

Fluttering her eyelids rapidly as she struggled to see Mr. Pat, Esabella moaned and mumbled something in a garbled whisper.

"Ah know, Butter Bean, ah know. It hurts like the dickens. I'll get that buzzard iff'en it takes me the rest of my life. I'll teach 'em ta mess with one of my young'uns." Mr. Pat sat back with a sigh and rubbed his eyes.

"She ain't really my own young'un, ya know," he said in a soft, emotional voice, "but me and Gertie raised all of them young'uns neigh-on eight years after thur' ma and pa passed on over from the yeller-fever. Otto, Annabelle and Esabella were some mighty fine young'uns. We all called Esabella Butter Bean cuz she loved those butter beans Gertie made." Mr. Pat shook his head wearily.

"But when Otto turned eighteen, he took the gals and moved on back inta that big ol' family mansion on Oak Street in Vicksburg. Now, Otto is a right nice feller and he took good care of our gals. Him and his Janie was a mighty good ma and pa to them.

"And now, little Annabelle has passed-on by some crazed man who dragged her off into a cave and now little Esabella is lying here pretty bad off herself from some crazed man. Land's sake, what is this world comin' to?" Lily, Ophelia and Mr. Porter

12

sat quietly for a few minutes as Mr. Pat rambled on a bit about Esabella.

"Well," he finally sighed, "Lily, jest make sure she don't fall off'en this hard bench and let me know iff'en her shoulder starts in bleeding somethin' awful."

Speaking in a soft, caring voice, Mr. Porter handed Lily a large, dingy handkerchief. "This ain't the cleanest but hit's the only'est thin' we got 'less ya got somethin' better to wrap around her shoulder and stop the flow of blood iff'en it starts up again. Do the best ya can gals, and we'll go kindly gentle-like with these mules." With that said, he and Mr. Pat jumped back up onto his seat and eased the mules forward.

"Ophelia, help me wrap this around her shoulder."

"Okay, I guess I can, now that I know she's alive and breathing… are you sure she's alive?" Ophelia stopped mid-step and waited for Lily's response.

"I have no idea. But let's get this handkerchief around her shoulder. Then we can ponder it," Lily said. She sighed as Ophelia shook her head in disbelief.

The handkerchief was as big as a baby's diaper, so they were able to wrap Esabella's shoulder fairly well. Afterwards they sat back and watched her sleeping body rock gently back and forth with the rhythm of the mules pulling them along the pitch-black trail, leading north towards Vicksburg Mississippi.

After a while, the air inside the stage seemed to thicken, making it a bit difficult for the two of them to breathe. Suddenly, the soft green glow reappeared above Esabella's head, and once again, twirled through the air and again took on the form of a woman, hovering above Esabella's head. The apparition wavered and floated for a long time before its mouth finally moved. As before, no audible sound came from the apparition;

13

Lily and Ophelia could hear its voice in their heads, "Find the murderer of Annabelle and Natty Bloome." is all it said.

Then, quicker than it appeared, the apparition vanished out the open window with a soft *swoosh*, leaving behind a trail of flickering green lights. The two girls stared silently out the stage window.

"Was that Annabelle Bloome?" Ophelia whispered to herself, "No, it couldn't have been… It said to find Annabelle's murderer!"

"No, it wasn't," Lily replied, still leaning across Ophelia to see out the window. "That was an apparition from a long time ago. Did you see the way it was dressed? It was dressed in clothes of like maybe… medieval times."

"Who is Natty Bloome?"

"He was Annabelle's husband. He was killed during the battle of Chickamauga."

"But the apparition said he was murdered!"

"Yep, it did," Lily mumbled.

"Well, what in the world was it talking about and why is it talking to *us*?"

"I don't know. Maybe Natty wasn't killed by the enemy during that battle. Maybe he was killed by someone else. We'll have to figure that one out, Ophelia," Lily whispered. She hesitated a minute before talking again. "We've seen some strange things in our adventures, but that was the strangest yet, don't you think?"

"Yes, it is," Ophelia replied, shaking her head in disbelief, still staring out the open window.

"Let's not say anything to Mr. Pat or Mr. Porter until we ponder on it some more," Lily suggested.

"Sounds good to me," Ophelia agreed, leaning back on the bench. "They'll think we're crazy."

After some time, Mr. Pat finally slowed the mules a bit, pulling the stage into a patch of tall pampas grass growing alongside the roadway. Gently he coaxed his team forward until they reached a man-made circle where he turned them around so they would be facing the trail when they left in the early hours of dawn. Lily cocked her head and listened closely. The forest was too quiet. Lily could read the signs a forest put out of a night. Forests were never quiet - not unless something strange was waiting to happen. Many times, she and Ophelia had experienced the movement of the night air when apparitions or spirits made their appearances. It was as if the night creatures knew all about spirits and haints and would hush their calling as they waited in anticipation; watching for movement in the spirit world which humans could not detect. Something was amiss in the giant, purple pampas grass; Lily could feel it deep in her bones. The apprehension tightened her muscles into knots.

Mr. Pat and Mr. Porter sat atop the stage, whispering softly before slipping quietly over the side of the stage and landing on the ground without a sound.

"Somethin's amiss, Porter," Mr. Pat muttered quietly outside the window. "I know it for sure."

"I'm thinking you're right," Mr. Porter replied. "I ain't knowing what it is, but somethin' ain't right in the night air. Should we move on out?"

"No," Mr. Pat whispered, *very* softly. Lily and Ophelia strained their ears to make out what he was saying.

Mr. Porter didn't wait long before speaking up. "What'cha thinkin' we 'aughta be doin'?"

"Well, ain't much we can do, Porter. We can't take the chance of running off the road with these mules and injuring Esabella mor'n she already is."

"Nope, we can't do that unless we have to," Mr. Porter whispered back as he quietly opened the stage door. He stuck his head inside. "Well, gals," he said, softly, as if to not awaken bad spirits, "I think we'll spend the night here. We can't see the trail anymore, and the mules might jest stop in the middle of the road and refuse to go another inch. You gals think you can jest' sleep right here on your bench? Jest' don't get alarmed iff'en we have to take off in a hurry. Okay?"

Both girls nodded their heads in agreement. Mr. Porter let down one of the window flaps and tied it securely to the bottom of the window.

Thick fog filled the small space among the tall grass where the stage rested. Giant, purple flowers swayed gently above their heads like a wavering wall, hiding them from prying eyes who might be coming along the road. The grass was so tall anyone passing by would not be able to see the stage or the mules. It covered the entire meadow except for the clearing which was thirty feet or so around. The forest started maybe fifty yards from where the stage sat, with mammoth oak and elm trees towering in the dark sky, reaching for the thousands of stars sparkling in the velvety black sky.

"Gals," Mr. Porter whispered as he leaned over the side of the stage, "iff'en either of ya need ta go inta the woods ta use the privy, don't be going alone. Let me or Mr. Pat know what'cha doin'. No telling what's out there in them grasses."

"Okay," the two girls answered nervously.

"I'm not using the privy, even if I bust a gut and wet my britches," Ophelia whispered to Lily. "Are you?"

"Nope, I'd rather wet my britches than go out into that tall grass. Something is out there...I can feel it in my bones."

"Me too," Ophelia whispered softly as she nervously looked out the window.

Leaning in close to Lily, Ophelia whispered quietly, "Like maybe that's where that green apparition came from. Or maybe something worse."

Without unhitching the restless mules or building a fire, both men stepped over their bench seat and laid down on the roof of the stage for the night.

"Keep the doors shut tight, gals," Mr. Pat whispered through a hole in the roof.

Too nervous to fall asleep, Lily and Ophelia sat on the hard-wooden bench, whispering and staring out the one open window at the fields of tall purple grass. A breeze was picking up and slowly blowing the fog out of the clearing. Heavy clouds drifted further to the east exposing the full moon which now lit up the open area.

Around about midnight, or so it seemed, thunder rolled far off in the western sky. Rapid flashes of heat lightning exploded in the distant horizon; these each lit up the clearing like daylight for a second or two. The lightning cracks subtly became more frequent; the thunder gradually grew louder. The girls in the stage, and the men up above all slowly became drowsy. After close to an hour, interspersed between the rolls of thunder, the girls heard the sound of the two men snoring loudly. Ophelia laid her head against Lily's shoulder, and was soon sound asleep with her mouth open, breathing heavily through her nose. She was almost snorting, Lily laughed to herself. Slowly, Lily's eyes also closed as she dropped into a fretful slumber as she sat straight up on the bench. Her head nodded and jerked; at some point her chin finally rested on her chest.

BOOM!

The earth shook from the force of the nearby lightning strike, jarring Lily awake. As the thunder rumbled and echoed, she jerked her head around to stare out the small window.

In those two seconds she saw it.

Standing at the edge of the grassy clearing was the black, shadowy form of a large man. Flashes of lightning revealed his terrifying silhouette. With the next flash of lightning, she saw the tall grass swaying around him, trying to hide him from her eyes. With the lightning behind him, she could see nothing but his dark shape. He was massive. Rapidly blinking her eyes, she leaned out the window a bit so as to get a closer look, thinking she may be dreaming, or maybe hallucinating.

Again, the lightning flashed sharply. The figure was gone! Each flash followed rapidly on the heels of the last, lighting up the clearing like a thousand candles in the dark. Her heart pounding in her throat Lily fretfully scanned her surroundings. The next flash revealed the frightening shape circling around the edge of the clearing, trying to approach the stage from a different angle.

Fear's icy hands reached inside her chest and gripped her heart; the blood racing through her veins seemed icy cold. Unable to move, all she could make herself do was watch as the silhouette loomed closer and closer. She opened her mouth to call out to Mr. Pat, but her voice was stuck in her throat. As she stared straightforward at the figure, she heard someone trying to open the tied-down window shade from the other closed window.

Realizing there were two of them, she twisted her head around to look at the closed window. Something was fumbling quietly with the knots. Reaching over her head, she grabbed the knocking stick and with a force never used before, slammed the stick against the roof of the stage and yelled out for Mr. Pat. The two men instantly began scrambling around the roof of the stage.

There came a loud *thud* and whatever was scratching at the closed window fell to the ground, bellowing loudly. But the figure in the tall grass was so close Lily could have reached out and touched it!

The stage jerked violently forward, knocking Lily sideways. Snapping his whip sharply above the mule's heads, Mr. Pat let out a loud roar to encourage his mules who were already jerking at the reins. At the same time, Mr. Porter cracked his own whip towards the creature. Braying loudly the mules heaved out of the clearing and jerked the stage onto the dirt trail. Just as the stage jolted forward, the creature's ashy, wet hand shot around the window, grabbed Lily by the throat, and flung her through the window and high into the air. Airborne, with eyes wide, she could see across the distant forest; she saw the entire meadow of pampas grass and beyond. As she began to fall, the creature flew after her, grabbed her upper arm while she was still midair, and with a sharp jerk, swooped down towards the stage and shoved her through the window. She landed with a loud thud between the two benches. She instantly felt searing pain in her shoulder and thought her arm may have been pulled out of its socket.

The beast, still at the window, looked inside for a moment. Pausing, it sneered, "I'll take the right one this time!" Its ashy hand reached for Esabella, as it snarled with anger.

CRACK! Mr. Porter's whip flashed through the air like a gunshot, and the creature shattered into a million pieces.

Not being able to contain her curiosity, Lily scrambled up from the floor, stuck her head out the window and watched as the shattered creature morphed back into a massive beast of a being. Again, Mr. Porter cracked his whip sharply, knocking the huge mass to the ground, where it then twisted and convulsed. It burst loudly into powdery ash, then immediately morphed into a dirty, grey wolf with a large gaped mouth, long fangs glistening in the moonlight and drool flowed from its jaws in ribbits. Rising on its haunches, it lifted itself into the air then flew right past Lily's face with a loud *SWOOSH!* Lily's hair blew away from her face as the wolf flashed by.

Shivering and clenching the armrest of the bench, fear seemed to wrap its cold hands around her throat and chest. It was difficult for her to breathe. She felt the creature's lingering sensation around her neck and on her arms. Frantically wiping her skin, her hands came away covered with sticky, black ash. It was as if the creature's hands had been burnt and were dripping some kind of nasty fluid. The putrid odor filled the stage, making it even more difficult to breathe normally.

Glassy-eyed and bewildered, Ophelia sat up and looked at Lily. She seemed confused. "What's going on? What is that awful smell?" Ophelia's body jerked back and forth with the jolting of the stage. "And why is your face covered in ash?"

"It was a shapeshifter," Lily replied, feverishly scrubbing at her neck. "I woke up and saw it coming out of the pampas grass, then Mr. Pat and Mr. Porter must have seen it too, because Mr. Pat cracked his whip and the mules took off. But that creature snatched me through the window, threw me up into the air, but then slammed me back into the stage when he realized he had taken me instead of Esabella!" Still shaking, Lily looked intently at Ophelia. "Then Mr. Porter cracked his whip again and the thing shattered it into millions of pieces! And then... then I watched it morph into a ghostly kind of wolf then it flew right past us; so close I could feel its whiskers on my face!" Another chill ran down Lily's spine as she recounted the story.

Rubbing her thumb down Lily's cheek, Ophelia quietly leaned over and whispered, "Obviously it has something to do with Annabelle, Natty, and Esabella."

"I'm thinking so too," Lily whispered, shaking her head. "Not unless it meant *you* when it snarled that he would 'get the right one' next time."

Ophelia jerked back against the wall, her jaw dropping all the way open and looked at Lily with wide-eyed horror, she whispered, "Me?" Why in the world would he want me?"

"I don't know, I'm just saying. It's either you or Esabella, because it didn't want me! But don't worry, I'm thinking it's Esabella, not you."

"Well, I sure hope so," Ophelia said in a squeaky little voice.

"Whoa!" The girl's conversation was interrupted by Mr. Pat calling out to the mules. "Slow up there, fellas! Did ya see that, Porter? That was a shapeshifter if I ever did see one." The mules did not seem to want to slow down. As he continued to work the reins, he turned and spoke back to the girls. "Lily, you okay girl?"

"I think so," Lily answered. "Just a bit frightened. That sure was strange. I've never had that happen to me before."

21

"Well, I ain't seen such like that before either. As long as you're okay, then we'll go on down the road."

"Sure was strange," Mr. Porter whispered as he shook his head. "What'cha wanting to do, Pat? Ya want to keep on going or do ya want to pull over up here a'ways and find us a good spot to stop fur' the night?"

"Well," Mr. Pat said, lowering his voice to a whisper, "I ain't never in all my born days seen a shapeshifter fling a young'un up in the air like that. I was plum scared myself! Let's ease on down the road a bit and maybe we'll come across Gator Brown's old cabin. He ain't gonna be caring if we spend the night. He hadn't been there in a month of Sundays and he's always told me to give 'er a try iff'en I'm on the road and need ta stop."

"Sounds good to me," Mr. Porter said quietly, his eyes darting from one side of the road to the other, watching for signs of danger.

The girls were feeling quite uneasy. They knew from experience that shapeshifters often return unexpectedly, and in any form they choose. Anxiously they stared out the window as the stage lumbered along the bumpy trail like an awkward, prehistoric dinosaur.

Finally, Mr. Pat eased off the road into another grassy meadow. Lightning continued illuminating the entire area as thunder rumble close across the black sky. Lily spied a tiny, run-down cabin sitting among a cluster of tall elm trees. Its only window was covered with gray, sagging, weathered planks of wood from years past; at least the door seemed to be intact. A worsening sense of unease rose in her chest again as she peered closely at the tiny dwelling. Even though it was small, the little cabin seemed unusually sinister. Ophelia wrapped her fingers tightly round Lily's arm; she too felt the disturbance in the air.

"I'm a little nervous," Ophelia whispered. "How about you, Lily?"

"Yes, I am, but Mr. Pat and Mr. Porter wouldn't have us stay someplace unsafe."

"Well," Ophelia said quietly as she sucked in a deep breath, "I hope you're right about that. But my mama always says at times men don't have the sense enough to come in out of the rain."

Quietly, with only the sound of the harnesses tinkling softly in the air, the mules pulled the stage to the front of the little cabin. Mr. Porter slipped silently down from his seat. The eight mules were nervously trying to step away from the cabin, but Mr. Pat held the reins firmly.

"I'll check it out, Pat," he whispered as he reached down and removed his heavy boots. "If I give a yell, 'jest take off outta here and leave me. I'll catch up with ya."

Speaking softly to the mules, Mr. Pat pulled the team around to face the road as he, Lily and Ophelia craned their necks around to watch Mr. Porter enter the cabin. Without a sound, Mr. Porter crept up to the small cabin and eased the door open.

Not half a minute later, out through the door flew Mr. Porter, his long legs churning up the dirt and his arms waving frantically above his head, signaling Mr. Pat to move out - and move out *quick*. Loosening his grip on the mules, Mr. Pat did not have to encourage the mules to move; he had to pull back a bit, or they would have taken off through the trees. Lily leaned her head out the window and watched as Mr. Porter sprinted the distance between himself and the stage. Without missing a beat, he caught up with the stage, reached up, grabbed the top rail at the back side and with a flip, pulled himself onto the top of the moving stage, scrambled to the front bench, climbed around Mr. Pat and sat down.

"Move out quick and quiet if possible, Pat." His tone of voice portrayed the need for urgency.

Once again, Mr. Pat snapped the whip above the mule's heads, but he did not yell out as he usually did. The team pulled them swiftly away from the disturbing little cabin.

No one said a word until the stage was a mile or so down the road. Eventually, Mr. Pat slowed the racing mules, and the girls could hear the men talking very quietly.

"It was the shapeshifter as sure as I'm sittin' here - and it was asleep," Mr. Porter whispered, leaning close to Mr. Pat. "It was changing back into a man, but the hind end was still that grey wolf. It looked to be, well, maybe..." he paused. "Maybe one of them fella's who had been burned up mighty bad."

Mr. Pat kept looking forward at the road. "You mean Charlie Juarez or Buster T. Tobin? Ya think so?" he asked quietly.

Mr. Porter lowered his voice even more. Lily and Ophelia leaned towards the hole in the roof so they could hear what he was saying. "For some reason my being there didn't wake it, but when I walked in its eyes was wide open and it was staring at the ceiling. It never did look at me. Ya think maybe it's one of them two fellas'?"

"Could be, Porter. Could be," Mr. Pat said softly.

Lily and Ophelia looked at each other, their eyes wide open. A deep-sounding moan coming from behind them made them jump and turn to see who caused it. It was Esabella. She was still lying down, but had opened her eyes.

Lily stepped across the narrow opening, sat down and helped Esabella into a sitting position.

"Mercy me, gals. I hurt like a son-of-a-gun; I don't think I'm gonna make it. Now, listen-up gals. Listen well." She held her hand over her chest and whispered, occasionally halting due to the pain. "When y'all get to Vicksburg, find Bob. He's Otto's boy. He has reddish-brown hair and blue eyes. He's about y'all's age, so he'll be easy to spot. He's usually amongst Otto's giant plants in the atrium, that's where he lingers most the time waiting for whatever it is he's waiting for."

Esabella sighed deeply, hung her head and gave a deep, rattling cough. It sounded as if her entire insides were coming up. "When you see 'em, make sure you get him away from anyone who might be around. Don't even say this in front of Otto. Keep it between the three of you." She paused again, wincing. "Good Lord on high, I'm hurting," she mumbled. Mustering up strength to speak, she said, "Tell him, 'det tage tre'". Her voice was soft. She then laid her head on Lily's shoulder and once again fell into a sound sleep.

....

Sitting on the hard, wooden benches, the two of them stared at Esabella, since there was nothing outside the window to look at but darkness and endless amounts of trees. Lily could feel her energy draining. It had been quite a night.

Sitting silently staring at Esabella, a soft, glistening green light once again slipped through the closed window and hovered above Esabella's head. It swirled gently into the form of a female then slipped quietly out the window again, vanishing into the night sky, leaving behind a long, stretched-out tail of flickering lights. Shimmering, it slowly faded into the horizon.

Fascinated, Lily rolled up the window shade so she and Ophelia could lean out the window to watch the flickering lights.

It looked like thousands of fireflies slowly vanishing into the velvety black sky.

"Mr. Patter," Lily called softly out the window, "I think Esabella might be gone."

Instantly he stopped the mules and the two men, once again, jumped to the ground and opened the small door. Jumping inside, Mr. Pat gently took Esabella's hand and held it tenderly in his own rough, weathered hands. Leaning down, he placed his ear onto Esabella's chest.

"It's faint," he whispered in a hushed voice, "but still beating."

"My sweet lass," he said, shaking his head with sorrow, "what has happened to our sweet, young, happy Butter Bean? Hang in there, child. Just a few more hours and we'll have you safely home. I'll find and get that damn creature - pardon me, gals - if it's the last thing I do." Emotion crept out through his voice.

Knowing time was not on his side, he slipped quietly out the door, climbed up onto his bench, picked up the reins and clicked to his mules. Lily and Ophelia eased Esabella back onto her bench and covered her with the well-worn stage blanket before leaning themselves against their own bench, where they sat and stared closely at Esabella's motionless body, desperately hoping she would open her eyes again.

All through the night, the stage swayed and rocked closer and closer to Vicksburg. The two girls dozed on and off in a fretful slumber, their bodies rocking with the rhythmic movement of the old, run-down stage. At one point, very late in the night, the tiny shimmering lights returned, slipping back through the window and floating around Esabella's prone body. Then, to the girls' surprise, the lights moved closer to *them*, glimmering and twinkling right in front of their faces. Was it trying to talk to them? After a brief moment, it floated out the window and vanished once more into the night.

2

The Old Mansion

Upon reaching Vicksburg, Mr. Pat urged the tired mules up Oak Street and came to a stop in front of a stately old mansion on the corner of Klein Street and Oak. With heavy, sorrowful steps, he jumped from the top of the stage and climbed the thirty-some steps to the front door of the veranda which stretched across the entire front of the house. This was called the Grand Corner Mansion. It faced the mighty Mississippi river as it rushed past Vicksburg on its way to the Gulf of Mexico to empty its belly.

If you could put its sinister mysteries aside, it was a wonderful house. Blooming blue and white honeysuckle vines meandered around the veranda pillars as they stretched toward the roof with tentacle-like fingers, each holding clusters of blooms that looked like clusters of grapes in a vineyard. The honeysuckle and ivy reached from one end of the veranda to the other - and beyond. Enormous Morning Glory vines, full of blooms, rose above the Honeysuckle vines, covering the entire right wall. The veranda looked as if it should be on the pages of a fairytale storybook.

Quietly opening the squeaky door of the old stage, Mr. Porter lifted Esabella into his strong arms, being careful not to bump her head against the doorframe. Carrying her, he led the way up the stairs. Lily and Ophelia followed them up the many steps to the magnificent front door, all the while staring in amazement at the majestic house. The front door stood ten feet tall and was made of solid oak. Colorful stained-glass panes graced either side of the huge door; hanging above the door frame was a brass plate with the address eloquently engraved upon it. Mr. Pat had already entered the house, and the door was now being held open by Esabella's brother, Otto. With watery eyes, Otto tenderly took Esabella from Mr. Porter's arms and carried her into the massive front bedroom, where he laid her on the enormous four-poster bed.

The house was deathly quiet and the air was cool as Lily and Ophelia stood awkwardly beside the front door, which was still standing open. They were waiting to be told what to do. The hushed whispers of the adults floated into the hallway.

"Everything here is massive... this hallway must be ten feet wide," Lily thought to herself as she craned her head around the hallway.

Easing the massive door shut behind her as quietly as she could, Lily then turned her head to the left and spied Otto, Mr. Pat and Mr. Porter along with two other adults - Josephine the cook and Mr. Kulicki the butler - gathered around Esabella, who evidently had not yet responded. Lily saw Josephine's eyes darting rapidly around the room; she quickly yanked her head out of Miss Josephine's view, but not before a chill shot up her spine.

Lily always felt uneasy around Miss Josephine. She was a strange creature. She was tall and elegant-looking, with a ram-rod straight back, and dark black hair pulled into a tight bun at the nape of her neck; her skin held the exotic tone of the Berbers from Libya and her coal-black eyes constantly shifted and darted about, recording each movement of every person in every room she happened to be. Even though she was well into her seventies, not a strand of grey hair graced her head. Whenever Lily had previously encountered Miss Josephine, for some reason chills would dance up and down her spine like a chicken dancing on a hot stove as those black eyes tried to find a way inside her very soul. It was as if Miss Josephine suspected something about Lily that Lily herself did not know. Each time she caught Miss Josephine's stare, she would quickly turn her head or leave the room. Lily occasionally caught a smirk on Miss Josephine's face after they locked eyes; it would send a ripple of goosebumps up Lily's arms.

Mr. Kulicki, on the other hand, was a kind, old gentleman; an Italian immigrant who had come to the States years ago. Lily met Mr. Kulicki when she was very young, and in her opinion, Mr. Kulicki had not seemed to have aged a single day since then. No one knew of Mr. Kulicki's family or where exactly he came from; all they knew was that he was born in southern Italy and fled his country in the late 1830's when the Austrian army invaded the Italian coast. He spoke with a heavy accent and was sometimes difficult to understand. He too had a dark, swarthy complexion and black eyes. Bushy, black eyebrows stuck straight up onto his forehead like feathers. Combining those with his coal-black hair, he could look quite ominous and at times even foreboding. He was a shadowy man, one whom Lily could very-well imagine slipping from one secret place to another, maybe from behind a hidden wall to a secret passageway, spying on everyone without anyone knowing.

"But," Lily reminded herself, "he *is* quite kind and gentle with everyone. At least as far as I can tell." He was definitely friendly, always bringing the children baked goods and the like from the kitchen. He would place whatever goodies he had snatched from the outdoor baking kitchen into their hands, and with a twinkle in his dark eyes, whisper for them to eat quickly so Miss Josephine would not catch them doing "such a deplorable deed", as she would say.

Esabella had previously told the girls the story of the day that Mr. Kulicki appeared. He approached the back door of the mansion on a cold, blustery morning when the sky was gray with heavy, wintery clouds and strong winds blew along the street. When Otto opened the door for him, Otto noticed quite a large flock of crows sitting on the fence-rail, just watching. It was unusual. Mr. Kulicki had bowed deeply and told Otto he had been "sent by fate itself" to watch over this old house and its inhabitants. He said he was quite sure Otto could use a fine, faithful butler, and if a place could be made for him, he would work for very little money. Immediately Otto whisked him inside the house, sat him in front of the roaring fireplace with a cup of hot brandy, and agreed to a fine arrangement for Mr. Kulicki.

Otto had later told Esabella that he had no idea why he brought Mr. Kulicki onboard, but his welcoming words seemed to flow right out of his mouth, without his brain giving any thought or input. Otto and his new butler came to "quite a fine agreement" that morning, and Mr. Kulicki had been with them ever since. Oddly, however, the flock of large crows, for some reason, also stayed around. In fact, they reappeared in the yard each time Mr.

Kulicki left the house and would follow close behind him until he reentered the house. "Very odd", Otto had always said.

Miss Josephine, who Lily considered downright spooky, had apparently come to join the growing household only a few months after Mr. Kulicki had arrived. According to Esabella, Mr. Kulicki was quite unhappy the day Miss Josephine appeared at the front door with her satchel. When Mr. Kulicki learned that Otto *hired* Miss Josephine, he was very displeased. But she had been referred to Otto by a dear friend, so Otto felt obligated to hire her. That was the only time Esabella had seen Mr. Kulicki frown. Esabella heard a quiet, angry sound coming from deep in his chest as he walked away after hearing the news. He later told Esabella that he did not trust or like this Miss Josephine right from the beginning, but that Otto *insisted* they give her a try since his dear friend Frederick had referred her to them.

It was rumored that at one point in her life, Miss Josephine had been a famous cook in the kitchen of a fine hotel in New Orleans, but ended up leaving because of the infamous voodoo woman, Marie LeBeau. Apparently, Miss LeBeau had taken a disliking to her and cast a voodoo spell on the restaurant, refusing to rescind it unless they released Miss Josephine.

The strangest thing about Mr. Kulicki and Miss Josephine was the time or two in which Lily had caught them standing alone in the large hallway between the parlor and the master bedroom, nose to nose. Standing very still, glaring silently at each other with hate in their wide-open eyes, it looked as though they were yelling at each other with their minds. As Lily peeked through a slightly open door, she had watched them for a good fifteen minutes just standing and glaring at each other. After a very long fifteen minutes of silence, Mr. Kulicki shook his finger in Miss Josephine's face and uttered in a hushed whisper, "Don't even *think* about it Josephine. You will NOT proceed with those thoughts of yours, or you will be extremely sorry." He then quietly slipped down the hall and vanished into his sleeping room. An evil smirk twisted onto Miss Josephine's face before she turned to walk the other way.

Lily had seen this happen a handful of times. In one such instance, Lily was peering through the crack in the door, and as Miss Josephine passed the cracked door, she snarled quietly, "Shut the door, you insolent brat!" Lily's blood froze in her veins, and quick as a flash, Lily shut the door and stood behind it, fully expecting Miss Josephine to come bursting through the door at any moment. But, luckily for Lily, she continued down the hallway and into the kitchen.

Thus today, Lily still felt uneasy around Miss Josephine.

Stepping to the opposite side of the wide hallway, Lily peered through an open door into the flower-filled parlor where the body of Esabella's sister Annabelle was laid out in her coffin. The parlor was overflowing with red, blue and yellow flowers, so much so that the casket was partially hidden from Lily's view. It looked like an indoor garden.

Lily elbowed Ophelia.

"Look," she whispered softly. "There it is again."

Ophelia craned her head around the parlor door frame and looked at the coffin. Hovering above Mrs. Annabelle's head were the same flickering, pale-green lights they had encountered on the road the night before. The two girls slipped soundlessly into the parlor and stood looking at Mrs. Annabelle as she lay in the beautiful coffin.

"What are you doing in here?" A sharp, angry voice snapped from behind them demanding an answer.

Startled, Lily and Ophelia jumped around to face an angry Miss Josephine. The flickering lights vanished with a nearly silent *whoosh.*

"Admiring the beautiful flowers," Lily said quickly in a timid, startled voice. "They are lovely, and Annabelle would not mind, I am sure." She forced herself to stare back into Miss Josephine's scary, black eyes. For a few seconds they held each other's glare until Miss Josephine muttered some unrecognizable words under her breath, and in a nasty, hissing voice ordered them to leave the parlor and not return.

"And in this house, you will address Esabella Bloome as Mrs. Bloome. That is, *if* you can find the manners, I am sure you have been taught!" she hissed.

Since Ophelia had never met Miss Josephine and had no idea about the kind of personality she was speaking to, she - quite unwisely - spoke up loudly. "Why?"

Miss Josephine had already turned to leave, but at Ophelia's question she whirled around making her black satin skirt swirl around her body as a gasp of unbelief burst from her mouth as if saying "How dare a child question her?"

"Because I demand it! And because there is no need for the two of you to be in the parlor! Now, leave this room and do as I have commanded!"

With that said, she turned sharply on the heels of her shoes and marched down the hall towards the kitchen. Lily and Ophelia heard the door to the small baking kitchen slam shut.

"Well," Ophelia whispered, "she's a mean one."

"You might say that," Lily murmured.

Peeking down the long hall towards the back of the house, Lily caught sight of a young boy with a big grin on his face standing at the other end. He stood quietly in front of a massive row of ferns and indoor flowering bushes growing along the large, glassed-in solarium. He could have been easy to miss since he blended in with the foliage. He raised a hand, beckoning for them to come towards him. Lily and Ophelia tiptoed quickly down the hall, glancing back to make sure Miss Josephine had not reappeared in the hallway.

The boy was on the tall side, with gangly arms like most young boys his age. His pants looked to be a mite short and his shirt a bit too big, but that was also normal for young, growing boys. Lily and Ophelia came to a stop in front of him, and for a good minute they stared at him and he stared back at them. He had reddish-brown hair and the strangest blue eyes they had ever seen on a human. His eyes reminded Lily of the blue eyes of a baby tiger she had once seen at the Boston Zoo when she was a small child.

He stood staring back at them silently for a bit before whispering, "My name is Bobby T, but you can call me Bob. I knew you were coming. Aunt Anna B whispered it to me no more than five minutes ago. Follow me - we have to get out of the house and away from these walls. They have unseen ears and eyes." Turning briskly, he walked through the back door into a garden.

Lily and Ophelia turned and looked at each other with surprise. Ophelia looked nervously up and down the wide hallway. "Ears and eyes?"

"I guess," Lily said, shrugging her shoulders.

The outdoor garden was a maze of hedges, brilliant flowering plants and trees of every kind imaginable. Stopping abruptly in front of a long, well-worn bench, Bob turned and looked at them. He whispered softly. "This is where Aunt Anna B would come to visit me when she was gone."

Ophelia looked Bob in the eyes. "What did you mean by 'unseen ears and eyes'?" She spoke softly, glancing around as if looking for conjured spirits.

Frowning, Bob looked at Ophelia. "You don't know, do you? This house has wide, hollow walls so folks can hide and listen to others, or sometimes, hide *from* others. During the war, many a person saved themselves by hiding in these walls, and others, well, they hid and never came out. Many times I have seen spirits slip in and out of the walls."

Ophelia swallowed hard as she turned and looked back at the doorway.

Bob continued on as if it were common for spirits to slip around his house. "When Aunt Anna B was gone on one of her many trips, her spirit would come back home and visit with me here in the garden. She had a special gift, you know. Just as you do, Lily Quinn, you also have a special gift. Your gift is being able to sense the spirits around you."

Lily swallowed hard and held back a small grimace. "Why would she tell you that?"

"Because," Bob looked at her and frowned deeply, "you do have a gift, but you won't believe it. Well, those are her words, not mine."

"You're strange, Bob," Lily whispered firmly. "I don't have a special gift and I don't want a special gift."

"Are you afraid of it?"

"Well," she paused, then continued firmly. "Afraid is a mighty strong word, but I'm not going to have anything to do with that leaving-my-body kind of stuff." Lily thought of their friend Tillie Brown and how she had left her body. Just weird.

Bob turned away from them, shrugged his shoulders and muttered. "Ok, that's up to you."

"Yep it is," Lily whispered loudly. "So, leave it be and don't mention it again."

It was silent for a moment. Then Lily remembered what Esabella had asked her to do. Standing in the middle of the grassy path, Lily tugged on Bob's shirt sleeve. *"Det tage tre,"* she whispered to him.

Whirling around, Bob stared at them wide-eyed, his mouth gaping open. Grabbing Lily by the nape of her neck, he quickly put his hand over her mouth. "Don't ever say that out loud around this house! Who said that to you?"

"Esabella did, right before she passed out the last time," Lily mumbled under Bob's sticky, sweaty hand.

Taking his hand away from her mouth, Bob grabbed both of their shirt sleeves and pulled them behind a thick Rose-of-Sharon bush. "Never, never repeat those words again as long as you are near this house!"

"Why?"

Bob did not answer Lily's question. Instead, he dug around in his pants pocket, pulled out a tiny stub of a pencil and a small scrap of paper. Holding the scrap of paper close to his chest he scribbled something then held it up for Lily and Ophelia to read. In messy writing, it said, *"Those words are from the crypt and could call up apparitions we don't want to encounter."*

Ophelia looked up at Bob and mouthed silently, "What?"

Bending down, Bob ignored Ophelia's question and began peering through the flowering bushes as he turned in a circle checking every spot in the garden. When at last he stood up, his voice was almost too low for the two girls to understand as he whispered. "Listen close," he said, cocking his head to one side to get a better listen. "I can hear it coming in the air. Can you hear it, Lily? It's on its way here."

"No," Lily replied.

"I can hear it. It's still a bit of a ways off but you will see it soon enough."

"Like… what kind of haints are you talking about?" Ophelia asked as she bent over and peered around the garden beside Bob. "I don't see anything."

Bob turned his head towards Ophelia and whispered, "You aren't using your eyes the right way. You have to squint your eyes half shut, concentrate on a specific area and then you can see it when it arrives. But sometimes you don't even have to try, it is as plain as the mud in a puddle."

"Just who are we looking for?" Lily asked as she too bent down and squinted, looking through the bush. Sure enough, Lily was sure she saw the air thicken and swirl.

Turning slowly, Bob spoke in a low, raspy voice. "Maybe Fartin' Freddy! Have you ever heard of him? He's a bad one. Maybe even Tuxedo Tom, or even worse, Toad-Frog Timmy, He's one of the worse haints there is around."

Lily and Ophelia both choked back a snicker. "Toad-Frog Timmy?" Ophelia blurted out with a laughing snort.

Immediately Bob whipped his hand over Ophelia's mouth. "Don't say that so loud, Ophelia! He might hear you and come running for us!"

She nodded her head in agreement, and Bob removed his hand. She whispered softly, "Who is Toad-Frog Timmy? Pray tell. Did he get bit by a big toad-frog when he died, or did he torture some toads and they pulled him into Toad-Frog world?"

Bob's face turned beet red as he glared back at Ophelia. "For your information, Miss Smarty-Pants, Toad-Frog Timmy is no laughing matter. I hear tell, from Aunt Anna B, that he tried chopping off the toe of a giant toad over in Africa where toads grow to be three feet long and two feet high, to get rid of a curse put on him by a witch doctor by throwing skeleton bones on his head. Well that toad jumped on him like a banshee and bit a hole right through his heart. I guess he dropped dead like a sack of potatoes and the folks with him couldn't find hide nor hair of his heart. All they could hear was his heart beating inside that giant toad-frog. He's mad, and he's a mean one 'cuz now he's in the afterlife with a skeleton stuck on his back because he couldn't get a toad's toe to dance the Red-Shirt Dance which takes away that particular curse. He's in a sad state of affairs, but it's no use now. He's stuck with that skeleton forever and he takes it out on every soul he runs into. If we see Toad-Frog Timmy, we're running the other way as fast as we can."

"Wait, wait, wait," Lily whispered as she turned and looked at Bob. "I've heard of Fartin' Freddy. In fact, we saw Fartin' Freddy floating down the Mississippi River not too long ago. My friend Katie Pirogue sees him all the time and he didn't sound like such a bad sort of fella - er, haint."

"Well," Bob hissed back, "he is now! I do believe he's the one who shot Aunt Anna B, I'm quite sure of it, or maybe it was that devil haint Tuxedo Tom. Whatever the case, if you two see them," Bob shook a finger in their faces, "don't let them see you and most certainly don't talk to them. Since the news got out that whoever finds the crown might get their human body back, all of them have gone bonkers. Both of them are now some bad hombres. You'll know Tuxedo Tom right off 'cuz he wears this raggedy tuxedo with a top hat and a dead rabbit hanging onto his leg." Cocking his head to one side as if hearing something neither girl could hear, Bob stopped talking and frowned deeply.

Then, without warning, the smell of putrid flesh swept into the garden; so thick it caused the Rose of Sharon blossoms to instantly wilt and fall to the ground. Bob hunched down once again and peered through the Rose of Sharon bush. "Holy Moly," Bob muttered under his breath.

"Come on, let's get out of here," he whispered. He stood upright and slipped behind a thick trellis of trumpet vines, pulling Lily and Ophelia along with him. "It's worse than I thought! It's one of those Gaggolang creatures. He must have heard you. Make yourselves invisible if you can."

Peeking through the trumpet vine, Lily stared at the main path of the garden. The air seemed to thicken as it slowly shifted and swirled. Then right before their eyes, a silvery outline of a creature pulled itself together from nothingness. The outline was barely visible. Only when the form moved could the three of them see its shape. Its silhouette had a silvery glow, but the rest of its body was transparent. When it moved, tiny sparks crackled and snapped off its outline. As its legs and arms moved forward, trails of shiny mist swept back like long hair until the form stopped and the thick, hair-like wisps caught up with its body and swirled around the creature like a swooping cape. Standing with their stomachs in knots and their hearts pounding loudly in their ears, the three of them watched as the creature turned its head in their direction and a large gapping sneer spread across its grotesque face.

Holding their breath, they pushed their bodies against the wall of the building as the creature turned its head and looked the other way. It was floating but seemed to be struggling a bit to pull itself and all the hair-like mists forward. Suddenly it stopped, leaned into one of the large windows of the house, raised its arms and peered inside. Out from its chest rumbled a deep, guttural growl, which evolved into a low, gravelly laughter that rolled up from its belly. It showered the large window in silvery spit with each deep laugh. The spirit then turned its massive head towards them again, and another wicked grin spread across its transparent face. It was horrifying. The beast had distorted facial features and eyes ablaze like the red coals from the fires of hades. In a voice echoing up from the depths of Hell itself, it raised its massive ugly head and bellowed. *"Bobby Tom… COME OUT TO ME!"*

Lily and Ophelia turned to look at Bob just in time to see him literally melt into the brick wall!

"Bob!" Lily hissed quietly. "Bob?"

All they could see was Bob's nose and chin as he eased himself into the wall, but then he was *gone*. With open mouths and bugged-out eyes, the two girls slowly turned their heads back to stare at the creature. It was staring directly at the plants in front of them. It raised its grotesque hand, pointed a long, silvery finger at them and laughed cruelly, before yelling out in its deep, hellish voice, *"Det tage tre, and now he has three!"*.

It whirled around, causing one of the long, shiny, hair-like tendrils to whip out toward the trumpet vine, where the tendril grabbed a hold of a vine and slowly wove its way closer to their faces. Pushing harder than ever, Lily and Ophelia pressed their bodies against the brick wall until Lily was quite sure her back would be scarred from the bricks.

The silvery wisp dropped to the brick pathway, slithered towards them on the ground and began circling Lily's right foot. Slowly it slid up to her ankle, then stopped; with a cry of rage, the creature jerked the wisp back to its body. Lily's heart jumped up into her throat. Neither girl moved. They held their breath as they watched the spirit. It seemed to be getting pulled into the sky by some unseen power. First its head elongated as if being wound around a pulley too high for them to see, after which its body was stretched paper-thin, thirty-some feet into the air, until - *SNAP!* - it vanished.

The girls sat down against the wall, astonished. Lily looked over to the house. In the oversized window, for a fleeting second before it disappeared, she saw something almost too faint to see - the angry face of Mr. Kulicki.

When the haint disappeared, it took its suffocating, putrid odor along with it. A soft breeze swept through the garden as hummingbirds returned to drink nectar from the trumpet vine blossoms. Scurrying from behind the thick vine, the two of them turned and stared at the wall where Bob had disappeared. The trumpet vine shook, quivered and rustled, then Bob stuck his head through the thick climbing vines.

"Is he gone?"

"Would we be standing here if he wasn't? Do we look like idiots?" Lily asked angrily.

"Is he gone?"

"Of course he's gone! What in the heck happened with you? And what was with that melting into the wall business? That was just too freaky for words, Bob."

"I told you to go into the wall, but you didn't seem to want to, so I went alone."

"No kidding!" Lily and Ophelia said at the same time.

"I do it all the time. You can do it too if you try."

"No, we can't!"

"Yes, you can."

Lily glared at Bob for a minute then turned away. "You are one crazy creature, Bob. Humans cannot melt into walls."

"Well, ever since I had the Pox, I can do all sorts of strange things," Bob said.

"Like melting into a wall?" Lily stammered.

"Yes, and I can also make myself invisible."

Lily and Ophelia stared at Bob intently.

"The Pox?!?" Ophelia whispered in a shrill little voice, backing up. "You had the Pox and lived to tell it? You put your hand over my mouth! That's not right, Bob! You could give me the Pox!"

Laughing, Bob answered her with a smirk on his face, "Don't worry, you can't catch the Pox from me. All the catching is done in the early stages."

Ophelia did not seem convinced. She gagged, spit, and wiped her mouth as much as she possibly could. "I'm thinking you're dead!" she stated matter-of-factly, still backing up.

"I'm NOT dead," Bob whispered loudly. "Grab hold of my arm. I'm a live person. I just don't know what happened when I had the Pox. It was kind of strange, ya know. One day I had the Pox and was lying in bed feeling like an eight-mule team ran me over, and the next thing I remember, I got up out of bed, all the spots were gone, and I could do these weird things like melting into walls and making myself invisible. It was the weirdest thing ever! The only people I told was Aunt Anna B and Aunt Esabella. They said to keep it to myself unless I really needed to vanish in front of someone. So, today was one of those times. I really needed to get away from that creature." He looked at the girls for a moment in silence.

"You didn't tell your Pa?"

"No, Aunt Esabella said he would worry himself sick, so I decided not to say anything to him about my powers. He doesn't have the gifts the rest of us have. He knows nothing about it so don't you two be blabbing it to anyone."

"Okay," Ophelia said in a squeaky voice. "I'm saying nary a word to a living soul."

"Neither am I." Lily said softly. "Now, that wasn't Fartin' Freddy, we know what he looks like. Who is this creature, and what in the world is a Gaggolang? And," Lily shook her finger at Bob, "don't you be lying about it!"

Crouching down among the peonies, Bob jerked Lily and Ophelia down beside himself. With a soft thud they landed on the damp wet ground.

"It's probably Dog-eared Dan. I think he's a Gaggolang. A Gaggolang is a person who's eviler than Hades itself even - after they die. I haven't seen Dog-eared Dan's spirit in a long time, and I hear tell he got what he asked for. Rumor is, he died when a pack of wild dogs gobbled him up like a pig eating slop. Now he's mad as a wet hen and out to get every soul he can get. But the rumor also says he deserved it. He was mighty cruel to his wife and kids. The wild dogs watched him from a distance for many a month, until one day while he was beating on his wife by the outside well, they attacked. Wasn't nothing left of him but his hair, and that was taken by a black raven who flew off with it hanging from its mouth. Even his bones were gone. Those dogs ate every bit of that fella and folks from all around weren't too sad about it a'tall. His nine kids were standing on the front porch watching the whole thing and nary a one could do anything since they were all too small. His wife, Polly, sat there by the well too weak from the beating to do anything to help hm but truth be told she probably didn't want to.

"At one time, before he became a Gaggolang, his ghost hung with Fartin' Freddy's haint, as well as Tuxedo Tom's. I don't know how a spirit becomes a Gaggolang, but it's a bad thing, they say, a very bad thing. There ain't a dead haint one who wants to end up being a Gaggolang."

Bob paused and looked them both in the eyes. "Now, I'm going to tell you both something, and it's never to leave this garden. Okay?"

The girls nodded in agreement.

"Way back in the late twelve-eighties there was a King of Wales named Llywelyn Gruffudd, and he was the very last Welshman to be king of Wales - ever! But, in twelve-eighty-four, old King Llywelyn was captured by the King of England, King Edward the - well, whatever his number was. King Llywelyn was taken, along with his jewels, treasures, and especially his valuable crown. The crown was originally forged from iron for King Borgward in the sixth century, then passed down and evidently ended up belonging to King Llywelyn. Well, King Ed took old Llywelyn and all his treasures to London, locked them up with the crown jewels in Westminster Abbey, threw old King Llywelyn into the tower of London and threw away the key. He even had the crown covered in gold to make it more suitable for England's treasury. But, nonetheless, the treasures were all stolen in sixteen-forty-nine by Oliver Cromwell during the destruction of the crown jewels. Well, lo'-and-behold, King Borgward 's crown was not present in the bounty, and 'til this *very* day, that crown remains hidden!

"Now, old King Llywelyn had one child, a daughter named Gwenllian-ferch Gruffudd. It's said she is the very one who stole her father's crown from Westminster Abbey right after it was taken by King Ed. From there she supposedly sailed away to the Americas on a Viking ship called *The Sea's Shadow*. Once she and her crew reached the Gulf of Mexico, they sailed all the way

45

up the Mississippi River and stashed the crown away in a hiding place known only by Gwenllian herself. Then she took her crew out into the Gulf, and quietly, one by one, the crew members vanished until all was left was Gwenllian. The story goes that she managed to lower a small boat into the water and from there she herself vanished into the wilds of America."

Hesitating for a few seconds, Bob swallowed hard and continued.

"And," Bob continued in an eerie whisper, "when the night sky is black as pitch and the moon hides its face behind the clouds, and the air becomes thick with sinister feelings of evil trying to grab your very soul, suddenly the moon will burst from its hiding place to reveal the thick fog covering the Mississippi. When you hear the howl of a wolf, it's then that you'll see it - *The Sea's Shadow* cutting silently through the night with billowing clouds of fog swirling around her hull. You watch with big 'ol eyes as she cuts along the bank of the river by the deserted docks of old Vicksburg. She drifts eerily along its edge, maybe as if looking for an opening that had once graced the edge of the river. Then, once again the lonely howl of the wolf echoes across the water, and just as quickly and quietly as she appeared, she vanishes into the fog."

Bob stopped talking and stared at the two of them for a moment before continuing his story in hushed whispers. "We can go tonight and see her if you want," he whispered softly. "I've seen her many a time; each time is just as frightening as the first."

Lily nodded yes. Ophelia nodded no.

"But, that's not the best part of the whole story," he continued. "This Gwenllian-ferch Gruffudd stayed in the Americas, married-up with a fella and had one child of her own.

It's said she never went back to get her father's stolen crown. On her deathbed, she whispered to her husband those three eerie words, *'det tage tre'*, then took her last breath and was gone into the great beyond. Her husband never did figure out what she meant and finally gave up his solo search for Gwenllian's pa's treasure. But as he lay dying, he too whispered those same words to his child as did every generation that followed.

"Well, on down through the years, Gwenllian's child married a Swedish woman and they had one child and that child married and so on and so on until the only living relative left of Gwenllian's descendants is none other than Pop, Annabelle, Esabella, and me! Can you believe that? Aunt Anna B told me the entire story before she passed on, and she told me how many folks, alive and dead, are hunting for the crown. The living folks want it for the gold, but the dead want it because it's said that if a dead soul finds it, as soon as he picks it up and places it on his head that particular haint will instantly grow flesh and skin and live forever.

"And that's why Aunt Anna B wants me and the two of you to find it for Otto and Esabella. Rightfully it belongs here in this house. I don't know why it takes three, but she said for me to never try and find it until two more came to assist me. So, I guess that's the two of you."

Sitting back on his heels, Bob stared at them intently, waiting for a reply. Lily scratched her elbow, as she always did when she was thinking, and Ophelia fiddled with her lower lip as the two of them contemplated the situation.

"Well," Lily whispered, "I guess it would be okay if Esabella and Annabelle wanted us to do it. What do you think, Ophelia?"

Frowning deeply, Ophelia glared at Lily before answering.

"I think I'm wanting to get out of here quick-like, Lily. Fartin' Freddy and Tuxedo Tom are no problem, but that Gaggolang we saw back there is a big issue for me. I vote for going home."

Far off in a distant section of the huge, dark garden, came echoes of deep laughter rippling through the air. "Come on, and be quiet about it," Bob said excitedly, not waiting for either of them to answer. Standing up, he looked down at their feet. "Take your shoes off." Quietly, Lily and Ophelia slipped off their shoes.

3

Skeletons

The day had now turned into night as they quietly but quickly tiptoed along the garden path until they came to a stop before an enormous wrought-iron gate leading into a private cemetery which was an extension of the gardens. The gate was rusty, but ornate; metal leaves and vines twisted and turned throughout its heavy metal spindles. Silently, the three stood looking through the old, weathered bars. Huge columns of damaged brick held the elaborate gate upright and a massive padlock kept it shut. On both sides of the gate, a brick wall towered over them and stretched as far as their eyes could see. Atop each supporting column sat a huge black bird with their heads cocked to one side staring directly at the three of them.

Bob, Lily and Ophelia could see into the cemetery through the gate's rusty spindles. Tall, rusty lampposts were scattered sparsely along a meandering brick pathway, their lit torches being pushed into small shadowy orbs by the thick darkness of the night sky. The path curved like a sleeping serpent amongst massive, overhanging trees and enormous headstones looming high above the earth. As they peered through the gate; their faces pressed into the gaps between the bars, the trees began to whisper and moan. The serpent-like path seemed to hiss as dead, dry leaves were pushed across it by a cool but gentle breeze. The weak lights from the lampposts flickered, seemingly losing their will to continue burning. Chills crept up the back of their necks as images of evil and unrest conjured themselves up in Lily and Ophelia's minds.

Trying to quietly take a few steps back and turn around, Ophelia had not made it but a few feet when Bob reached out and grabbed her arm. "Come on, Ophelia, we need your help! It's not as scary as it looks."

"I know," Ophelia replied softly, jerking on her arm to get away from Bob. "It's scarier than it looks!"

"No, it's *not*," Bob whispered, holding her arm firmly. "Come on, let's go in!"

Reluctant, Ophelia stayed put. "We can't get in. Do you have a key? That rusty old lock is holding the gates shut!"

"Yes, we can," Bob replied. "I can help."

Bob slipped through the narrow spindles with ease as Lily watched the solid metal give way to his body.

"Strange," Lily whispered to herself. "That's just too creepy, Bob."

He reached back through the bars, grabbed Ophelia's arm, gave it a quick yank and instantly she too was on the other side. Lily noticed that Ophelia's face had gone ghost-white, and her mouth was hanging open; she looked obviously startled but didn't seem to be in pain.

"Okay, now it's your turn, Lily," Bob whispered over the sound of the trees.

Lily put one leg between two spindles, but, as much as she concentrated, the rest of her body would not go through. Reaching out, Bob grabbed Lily's hand, and with a little yank pulled her through. with no problem whatsoever.

"See? No problem whatsoever," Bob whispered. "But you need some practice, Lily."

"How did you do that?" Lily asked, astonished.

"I dunno, it just happens!"

Lifting a finger to his mouth to tell the girls to be quiet, Bob turned, stopped, bent down on his knees and peered through the trees.

"Come on!" He whispered, motioning with one hand.

A milky white fog swirled across the cemetery lawn; cool to touch, it sent chills down Lily's spine. She took a deep breath to shake it off and followed closely behind Bob as he walked down the path without making a sound. Slowly and silently, the three of them crept through the fog along the winding path for quite some time, occasionally disturbed by the creaking and moaning of old trees and the snapping of a dead branch in the wind.

After what seemed to be half an hour, the disturbing sound of laughter cut through the air, and all three of them ducked behind whatever they were close to. Bob dove behind a bush, Ophelia hid behind a tree trunk, and Lily crouched behind a tombstone. Time seemed to stand still; the only thing Lily could hear was the rustling leaves in the trees and her heartbeat in her ears. Lily made eye contact with Bob and Ophelia; Ophelia looked uneasy to say the least, but Bob seemed to be holding himself together.

Stopping to peer from their hiding places, they caught a glimpse of a huge fire flickering in the dark wooded area of the cemetery, still quite a bit ahead of them. Bob motioned for the girls to follow him. Coming out from behind the bush, he crossed the brick pathway and headed into the darkness under of the trees. Lily and Ophelia stayed immediately behind him, uncomfortable with the idea of being separated from him.

Finding an opening through which he could spy on whomever was gathered around the fire, Bob whispered under his breath.

"*Spectre de Rencontre...*"

"What?" Lily whispered, leaning in close.

"*Spectre de Rencontre* - it's a ghost rendezvous. I always thought it was somewhere around our house, and now I've found it!"

He chuckled deep in his chest. "Every other time I searched; I came up empty handed. All I ever found was smoldering embers of a fire. But now - now I've found it!"

Silently, Bob led them even closer to the fire until they came within fifteen or twenty feet of it. They stopped behind the trunk of a giant elm tree. Ophelia knelt on the ground to peer around its massive trunk while Lily and Bob craned their heads carefully around either side. Two figures were sitting comfortably around the fire.

"Ghosts," Bob whispered.

Lily knew differently. Two flesh-and-bone men were sitting around the blazing fire, and Lily recognized them both.

"They're not ghosts," Lily whispered quietly in Bob's ear. "That's Chauncey Jenkins and Shadrack Jones!"

"Well, horse feathers!" Bob whispered under his breath. "Where's that dang *Spectre de Rencontre*?"

Ophelia snickered quietly under her breath. Turning to Bob, she whispered, "I know old Shadrack Jones. He's the biggest chicken-liver I ever did see. I bet if we jumped out at him, he'd jump up and start screaming like a girl. I'm surprised to see him out here at all! One time, my little cousin Nattie chased him off our land with a snake made out of wood chips."

Ophelia and Lily laughed quietly.

"Well don't do anything to chase them off. Let's hear what they have to say," Bob hissed. "Who's this other fella?"

"Chauncy Jenkins is from Hogs Hollow, Tennessee, but Shadrack Jones is from Caruthersville! These two spend most of their time together with the other railroad hobos who lounge around the train depot and sleep under its platform. They sure ain't haints," Lily whispered. "They hang out at the train depot 'til Pete Turnkey, the ticket master, chases them off and they wander on down to Ms. Bertha's café for a free cup of hot coffee."

"Dang," Bob whispered. "I thought for sure we'd found the rendezvous place."

"Nope, they're flesh and bone. And, come to think of it, Sheriff Beaumont is looking for these two something powerful. I guess they tried robbing a payroll train by pulling a wagon load of horse manure onto the tracks, but when that big old locomotive hit that wagon, the whole thing shattered into a million pieces, manure shot into the air like an explosion and covered the two of them from head to toe! Sheriff Beaumont was riding in the locomotive with the engineer when it happened, he saw it all! He said when he and the engineer saw it, they couldn't stop laughing. I guess Chauncey and Shadrack took off running down the tracks covered in manure like the devil himself was after them. Instead of getting the payroll money, all they got was a backside full of buckshot - the engineer shot at them with his shotgun through the window!"

The three of them snickered quietly as they imagined Chauncey and Shadrack running into the woods covered in manure and high stepping it to avoid the buckshot.

The two men were now leaning leisurely against logs, relaxing like they had the world by its tail and didn't have a single care on this earth. Chauncy had an old, felt hat pulled low on his head; it looked like he was trying to hide his face from other folks. His left leg jerked continually, ever since he'd been kicked by a mule as a kid. So now, his foot was bouncing back and forth, into and out of the flames. Chauncey was a long, tall, skinny fella with skin as brown as a walnut. He had the long, straight nose and high cheekbones of the local Kickapoo tribe; and his arms and legs were long and lanky too, making his torso look too small for his body. His black hair hung in greasy clumps about his face and shoulders in a thick, messy mass. His teeth seemed to be larger than what his mouth was made for, so when he smiled (which he did continuously) his teeth seemed to almost pop right out of his lips. They reminded Lily of horse teeth - but greener, and definitely more gross. His goofy smile was big and wide enough for a person to see every last one of his 32 teeth, but Lily was quite sure he had more teeth than the normal person. The strangest thing about Chauncy Jenkins, though, was his Adam's apple. Even though it was huge, it would disappear every time he smiled! Sometimes at night, if he was walking along a dark country road and came upon another person, he would bug out his eyes and smile *real* big, knowing it would give the other person's heart a flutter.

Watching Chauncy walk or run was an event in itself. When he walked, his shoulders would hunch over and his legs would take long strides out in front of his torso, as if his legs were trying to leave his body behind. Sometimes it looked like the lower half of his body arrived at his destination before the upper half. For some reason, whenever Chauncy walked or ran, his leg muscles did not jerk and twitch, but his neck and head moved forward in rhythm with his long legs, almost like his head provided the pushing power for his feet. His arms were always bent at the elbows, and with each step, it looked as if he were reaching out for something. He reminded Lily of the wheels on a locomotive, his arms being the turning arms of the giant wheels that pushed the locomotive forward.

Shadrack Jones, on the other hand, was a short, pot-bellied fella with legs the size of tree trunks, and a voice that was surprisingly deep for a short man. Every time Lily had seen him, he had been wearing the same britches and shirt. His face was constantly beet-red, his eyes were a gun-metal grey, and his hair was as white as snow. Folks from Caruthersville would say Shadrack was born with hair as black as a raven, but when he was delivered by the old midwife and he opened his eyes, the sight of that ugly, old woman scared the color right out of his hair!

A few years back, when Lily, Ophelia and the Pruiett boys were in Memphis, they saw Shadrack at a country fair trying to win some money by singing. His voice was deep, and he carried a wonderful melody; he mesmerized the crowd with the emotion in his voice. They were positive Shadrack would easily win the prize money. However, the town mayor's skinny little daughter won, even though she couldn't sing a lick. Everyone knew it was a sit-up deal. Well, the next day, word got around that the mayor's daughter's winnings had went missing. Lily had a pretty good idea who actually ended up with that ten dollars.

Shadrack's mother Hattie had come from a wealthy farming family, but Shadrack had no desire to live in the lap of luxury. As adults, whenever any of his six sisters saw him in town, they would turn up their noses and look away, acting as if they had not seen him. They would even cross the street so they wouldn't have to pass him on the sidewalk. Shadrack was the same way, if not worse. If he spotted one of his sisters in town, he would go out of his way to walk close behind them, mincing along and mimicking the way they walked, prancing and swishing his hips in great exaggeration, flipping imaginary hair away from his face with his nose stuck high in the air.

The only sister who acknowledged Shadrack was his little sister Nicolette. Nicolette would run up to Shadie, as she called him, give him a hug and say, "Shadie, you smell like horse manure. And you should stop being a brat!" They would both laugh, and he would tell her she was "a cute little tyke", even though she was almost thirty years old and married with two children of her own. Several times, Lily had noticed her slip something into his britches pocket and go her own way. Lily knew Nicolette was giving him money, because one time, some of the coins slipped through a hole in his pocket onto the walkway. Lily had hurried across the street, picked up the coins and chased Shadrack down, telling him he had lost a few coins. He grinned broadly at Lily and gave her a big wink and said, 'Shhh, 'tis a secret!'

However, once Shadrack took up with the hobos hanging around the trains, he never went home to see his family again. He might have gone to see Nicolette, but if he did, Lily never heard of it.

***

"Did I ev'ah tell ya 'bout the time me and ol' Jubal Early were down in ah boneyard in Lafitte, Louisiana, digging up graves and finding trinkets and the like?" Shadrack spoke in a low, quiet voice. He lowered his head and darted his eyes around the forest, making sure no one else could hear.

"Nope, never did, but I'd like ta hear ya tell it. Iff'en ya found something valuable down there, maybe we 'otta start-in digging up some graves here," Chauncey whispered back as his leg jumped into the fire. Sparks sprayed up higher than the men's heads before his leg jumped back out.

Chauncey too peered around the forest then admitted one of his own crimes.

"Once, a mighty long time ago, I dug myself up a grave and took a gold coin as big as my fist off this here rich fella's neck, then real quick-like I slammed that coffin lid shut and took off running for the hills. I was sure that fella's dead bones was gonna jump up and citch' me, but they din't. Well, I don't know iff'en they jumped up or not, but they sure din't citch' me," he said. He paused for a moment, looking into the fire. "So, did you and ol' Jubal find any gold or silver?"

"We did find us some gold," Shadrack replied as he sat up straighter and leaned toward his friend, still using his whispery voice. "And that ain't all we found. We found ourselves some gen-u-wine' haints! Hit was almost the scariest durn thing we ever did find... 'ceptin' the time we hear'd the good Lord himself yell out and tell us to put ol' widder' Haines' money back inta the bag she dropped on the roadside.

"But anyway, we'd heard about this rich feller dying, a feller who had went out to Californy and struck it rich in the gold mines when he was only into his twenties. Turns out he'd been orphaned as a young'un, and then when he came on back to Naw'lins with all his gold, he still din't have nary a single soul of a family, cuz' his wife and young'uns had all passed on while they was in Californy. So, when he died, the town folk of Lafitte was huntin' fur his relatives, and we heard about it. So, we jumped on the train to Naw'lins, where John P was living before he died and borrowed an old mule to ride over to Lafitte where they was having the buryin' ceremony.

"Then we got ourselves all gussied up and went on out to this Mister John P. Rousse's buryin'. We told all them rich folk we was John P. Rousse's long-lost uncles. You see, we found out he was orphaned back when he was a young'un – I guess his ma and pa died in a fire way out in the wilderness as they was traveling with a small wagon-train, comin' to Memphis from somewhere out west. Evidently, they had lost ev'rything they had in the gold mines or something like 'at.

"It's said they was travelin' durin' a storm, so them folks found an ol' abandoned barn and got all huddled inside 'til the storm passed. Well, then John P's ma put him in a box with a top on it and put him outside so he could get some fresh air while the rest of 'em gathered up all their belongin's they had left inside that old barn, but then the fire started and it went so quick and burned so fast that the ol' barn collapsed and locked ever' last one of 'em inside. Them folks din't have a chance to escape.

"Well, the story is that little John P. stayed in that box crying for days until another wagon-train came along and they found ol' John. With him a letter with his name on it and addressed to an old woman in Naw'lins who, unknown to them, had passed on a month or so beforehand. When that wagon master got to Naw'lins, he couldn't find hide nor hair of that ol' woman's relatives, so John P. was given to a young couple to raise as their own. 'Tis a mystery how John P's ma knew to put the letter in the box, but she did somehow.

58

"Well, me and Jubal missed the actual funeral, but we made it to the after-buryin' shin-dig and found out just where old John P. was buried. We introduced ourselves to ever'one as Shadrack and Jubal Da'dabber and told those folks we were mighty sorrowful that we missed John P's funeral 'cuz we had a mighty hard time finding out where it was, us being from out of town and all. Well they were mighty interested in knowing who John P's ma and pa was, 'cuz they din't know nary a single thing about 'em. Even John P. his 'self din't know a single thing 'bout his ma and pa. So, we goes on and tell 'em all these big tales 'bout Sari and her husband Hank, and they fall for it, hook, line and sinker! We told 'em how we had been searching for our sister Sari and her husband for many a year but never did find out what happened to 'em until we saw John P's picture in the paper and realized it was their son. We told 'em he was a spittin' image of his gran'paw."

Shadrack paused and chuckled, still looking at the fire.

"What?" Chauncey asked.

"Well, old Jubal, you know him and his bawlin'. He turned them tears on and sobbed like a baby, right there in front of all 'em folks. He was sniffing an' wiping snot 'til I almost told him to shut it off. But them women-folk took to him like flies on horse dung and started in hugging on him and took him by the hand and led him to the eating table where they found us a spot right in front of all that food. They treated us like royalty! They wanted to know all about John P's family, so we made up some whoopers of a few stories, then they wanted to know what John P's real name was and we stammered around a bit trying to think of a good name, but we acted like it had just been *so* long we couldn't remember it right off hand, that we all just called him 'Baby' for such a long time. But then Jubal shouted out that John

P's real name was Abner Dubois. Well, them women-folk got all teary-eyed and said that was the sweetest name they ever did hear, and one o'dem young women said she was gonna name her next baby Abner Dubois 'cuz it was 'a fine, upstanding name', and the men folk, right away, got a fella to carve *ABNER DUBOIS* right under *JOHN P. ROUSSE* on the gravestone.

"We ended up sittin' 'round that eating table for neigh-on three hours, makin' up stories about our sister Sari 'til we plumb ran out of made-up tales. Them folks hung on ever' word like it was the gospel truth, too. Eventually, when folks started in leaving, this here widder' woman Ms. Wilson insisted we stay with her for the night. She had sat there on her rocking chair the whole afternoon with a scowl on her face, eyeballin' ever' lady who talked to Jubal. Well, when she invited us to 'er home, a shiver ran down my spine like the devil himself was dancing a jig up and down my backbone. I must'a looked perty uneasy, cuz' all the folks 'round us said she was the best woman in town and would treat us mighty fine. In fact, they pulled me and Jubal and purt-near carried us to the widder's house! So, we agreed to stay with 'er, but right before we left, a feller' pulled me aside and whispered in my ear. He told me, 'Widder Wilson is eyein' Jubal as her next husband, and she's done gone through five of 'em before, and ever' one of 'em died in 'er house from fallin' down the stairs!

"Well, we walked into Widder Wilson's cold, eerie home, and she showed Jubal into this here big, old, fancy room with all kinds 'a doo-dads sittin' around, and she kindly *shoved* me into a little-bitty room not much bigger than a water closet. She threw a long men's night shirt in after me and sternly told me to leave my clothes outside in the hallway so I wouldn't get germs on her bed linens. Now, I knew she had more bedrooms than that little water-closet sized room, 'cuz that house was the biggest house I ever did see in all my born days!

"Well, long about midnight or so, I was still sitting in that cramped-up, tiny little bed, just wide-awake, too scar't to fall asleep. So, I decided to get up and have a peek outside into the hallway, still wearin' that long night-shirt she'd gave me. Even the hallway was full of valuable looking doo-dads! I was sure I could stuff some of them things into my britches' pockets if I put my clothes back on, but when I looked down to pick up my shirt and britches, they was gone! Then I hear'd a noise comin' from down the hallway, so I jumped back inta that room and in a flash dove inta the bed! Lo' and behold, there was Widder Wilson! She stood thur' at the end of my bed with her arms stretched out like a voodoo woman or somethin', and she says to me in this scary, deep voice straight outta' Hades, 'You are a liar from the depths of Hell, and I will send you back to the lake of fire for the lies you are telling!'

"Well, my eyeballs popped out of my face and I jumped right up out of that bed, flung open the door and raced into Jubal's room, where lo' and behold, thur' stood Widder Wilson at the foot of Jubal's bed, kinda like thur' was two of her making moon eyes at Jubal like she really, really liked 'em or somethin'! She was flappin' her hair from one side of her head to the oth'ern while smilin' and a'grinnin' at 'ol Jubal! He was shaking so hard his cover blanket was flapping in the breeze."

"What'd ya do?" Chauncey whispered.

"Well, I gave out a yell, which got her attention. I held up my hands in the sign of a cross and instantly her face turned into the face of a witch! So, I reached across that big old bed, grabbed Jubal by the arm, and like a far'fly flash I drug him out of that room, down those big old steps and out into the widder's yard. I was sweatin' like a mule trying to haul an elephant. When we got out onto the road, we stopped to look back at that house, and ever' winder in that house was lit up like a Christmas tree. I swear to my dying day, there was spirits shooting out that front door in groups of three and four with their mouths hangin' wide open and big ol' black holes where their eyes should'ah been!"

A branch fell out of a tree not too far away from the two men, who both jumped a little, obviously startled. The cool night breeze made the trees whisper around them, almost as if they were talking to each other about Shadrack's story. It made the two men feel a little uneasy. Their fire crackled a little louder and glowed a little brighter from the wind. Lily, Bob and Ophelia leaned in to listen more intently.

"So how-how-how'd ya get the gold?" Chauncy stammered, his eyes bugged out, darting around nervously.

"Well hold on a sec," Shadrack frowned, not as nervous as Chauncy. "Don't get ahead of me now. So, what was I sayin'," he paused? "Right. Well we know'd we had to get rid of those nightshirts and get our clothes back, so we snuck around the bushes to the widder's backyard, and what do ya' know, she'd done thrown all our clothes out the bedroom winders! So, we scrambled over, picked 'em up and changed our clothes right there in the moonlight with all them night critters a'watchin'. When I got fully dressed, I realized she'd kept my rabbit's foot! I guess she didn't want us to have any good luck. Well, she was wrong!

"We nosed 'round in her barn and found us some shovels, then high-tailed it back to that boneyard where old John P was buried. Real quiet-like, we slithered from one gravestone to the next until we found his fresh-dug grave. But perched right there on the top of his big, old headstone was the ghost of a pretty young woman in a long, flowing haint dress that was blowin' gently around her legs in the night breeze.

"Well, me and ol' Jubal froze right there in our tracks and stood just as still as one of them there headstones and watched her. She was kneelin' down with her head close to John P's grave; it looked like she was weeping. As if this scene weren't crazy enough, then up outta that grave came the ghost of old John P himself! But he was jest' a babe! Once he rose on up outta there, the woman stood up and grabbed holt' of that baby haint and started in weepin' loud!

"Well, me and Jubal was watching both of them real close-like, and with the moon being so bright, we could see their faces as clear as day. Then in a soft, kinda motherly voice, I heard 'er say, 'My baby', and then the baby haint started callin' out for 'er. It was darn near the weirdest thin' I ever did see. But then, just as quick as a flash, both of 'em vanished into the stars and the boneyard went back to nothin' but the sounds of the night.

"Now, that was pretty dang frightenin' thing right there, so me and Jubal stayed put for a good ten minutes until Jubal said he thought they was gone for good. We creeped slowly over to the grave and waited a bit longer, nervously fidgettin' a bit, then started in digging."

Shadrack leaned further over the fire as he whispered quietly. "It was almost like them graveyard trees was bendin' down close to us and frownin'! Them owls stopped hootin' and nary a cricket was chirpin'. Even the bull frogs in the pond shut up their croakin'. Gooseflesh popped up on my arms and I got the heebie-jeebies. Somethin' was wrong - I could feel it in my bones. But Jubal wasn't bothered a'tall, so I let him to start in the diggin' and I swallered my fright. It didn't take long to see John P's coffin, since the ground was fresh dug and all. So, I jumped on down with Jubal and we commenced diggin' out the coffin. I don't know what his coffin was made of, but it was black and as shiny as the hearse that carried it to the boneyard. We stood there for a minute just starin' down at it then Jubal grabbed ahold of that fancy, black handle and gave it a hard pull. It didn't open on the first tug, so he gave it another go, then *POP!* The seal broke.

"Just as soon as the top half of that coffin creaked open," Shadrack continued, "the moon sent down this here bright beam of light shining right smack-dab on the face of that dead man's mug, makin' it just as clear as if it was daylight. He had his top-hat on, with white gloves and the finest suit I ever did see. At first, I thought I saw his eyes open, but I knew I was just imaginin' things. But when I looked again, his eyeballs had popped wide open in the moonlight, and a smirk had spread across his dead face! It was the scariest thing I ever did see I tell ya! Outta the belly of his chest rumbled some deep groanin' words, 'Ma told me you were coming,' or somethin' like that he called out in his croaky dead man's voice, then lifted one cold, fleshy hand and grabbed ahold of Jubal's arm like he was gonna drag him into the land of the dead, but then he closed his eyes, let go of Jubal's arm and started snoring! It was the craziest thing!

"So, real quick-like, Jubal reached down and grabbed John P's gold pocket watch and I snatched some gold pieces that had fallen out of his breast pocket. Then we jumped out of that hole and took off running like there was no tomorrow! We heard the creak of a coffin lid slam shut, and without stopping, we turned our heads to look back. All that dirt we had shoveled out was flying through the air right back into that hole - *with nary a soul shoveling!*"

Impressed with his own story, Shadrack looked at Chauncey, waiting for his response. Chauncey looked him dead in the eyes and said nothing. Realizing he was supposed to say something, Chauncey spoke up.

"That's all the gold ya got?"

"Well, hold on a sec," Shadrack replied impatiently. "Suddenly, up from the bowels of Hell came this here black voodoo wind. It swooped down upon us like a hungry dog! We heard it moaning and howling all 'round us, and we felt it rip and tug at our shirts and our britches! We had our heads down and we hung on tight to each other, or we'd ah' been blown right down into that fiery furnace itself – that I know'd for sure. But that wind was so strong, we started tumblin' and rollin' along that road like ah' big old ball of mankind. After a bit, that black voodoo wind blew us straight into a big, fallen tree trunk, where I grabbed a'holt of a branch so me and Jubal could hang on for dear life. Jubal swears he saw one of them voodoo witches in the midst of that wind, cracking a whip and urging that devil's wind into a frenzy. He said her mouth was wide open and her teeth were shinin' like chunks of burnin' coal! He said 'er hair was black as midnight and it was flying around like a top, spinnin' right on the top of 'er head!"

Shadrack realized his voice had grown loud from his excitement. He took a second to settle down again. Whispering, he continued.

"After a bit, that wind blew us purt' near all the way under that fallen tree. Branches and leaves and entire *bushes* was flying past us! That witch woman kept right on howling and whipping the wind around like a bullwhip. It purt-near sucked the breath right outta' my lungs and I was gaspin' for air! It was evil, I tell ya, Chauncey. Pure, dog-gone evil."

Shadrack stopped talking and sat in silent contemplation. A moment later, he shook his head, and with glassy eyes he mumbled under his breath.

"Wha'd you say, Shadrack? I couldn't hear ya," Chauncey whispered.

Shadrack kept looking straight at the fire with glassy eyes.

"It was the Voodoo Witch-Woman, I tell ya. I know'ed it right off," he said.

"Well, come on, come on!" Chauncey demanded to hear the rest of the story. "What'ja do then?"

Shadrack looked at Chauncey with a surprised face, as if he hadn't seen him there for quite some time.

"Oh yeah, sorry. I forgot ya was sittin' there, Chauncey."

"Well?"

"Right. Well, we was thinkin' she must'ah lost sight of us when we was hidin' under that big ol' fallen tree, 'cuz away she went into the sky with that devil wind trailing along behind 'er. Once she left, the night turned as quiet as any other night would be - jest the cricket's chirpin'.

"Still twitchin' in our britches, we crawled out from under that tree. We figured we'd managed to escape from three evils that night already – Widder Wilson, John P's dead-but-livin' body, and now the Voodoo Witch Woman – so we must have some good luck. Looks like it's luckier to have your rabbit's foot stolen than it is to keep it!

"'So, with this much good luck behind us', we told ourselves, 'we might as well go on back to the boneyard and find some more gold since it's a boneyard for *rich* dead folks. Shakin' off our fears, we slithered and slipped from tree to tree again until we were back inside that boneyard. After checkin' to make sure no one was around – flesh or haint – we started lookin' for a good grave to dig. The first good lookin' one we came upon was the grave of a Mrs. Celeste Bonette. I know'd right away who she was. She was the wealthy wife of a sugarcane plantation owner. She'd died giving birth to the last of her *twenty-one* young'uns. Twenty-one! Can you believe that, Chauncey? So anyway, we slipped quietly back to the grave of old John P, cuz' we needed our shovels back. When we got there, it looked the same as it had a'fore we dug it up earlier! It was freshly packed, all professional-like. It gave me some serious heebie-jeebies, so we picked up our shovels and hustled right back to Mrs. Bonette's grave.

"So, you know, we dug up her coffin, and just like we thought, it was choke-full of gold and jewels. I mean, *choke-full*! Jubal grabbed all the gold around her neck and I snatched up the jeweled rings on 'er little bone-fingers and out we jumped to take off. I had all those rings in my britches pocket, but Jubal – he neva' was the smartest - had all those gold chains around his neck and was clinkin' and clankin with ever' step he took. We got half-way outta' that boneyard when, all of a sudden, right there in front of us was the haints of Mrs. and Mister Bonette themselves! Old Mister Bonette had his boney hand stretched out, pointing at the gold chains hangin' round Jubal's neck. Then in a flash, Mister Bonette had his haint-hands around Jubal's neck, trying to choke him! But Jubal reached up, and pulled the haint's arm up and away, and that boney arm broke at the wrist! But the skeleton-haint hand kept right on grabbing and snatching at Jubal's neck!

"But *then*," Shadrack said with a dramatic voice, "Mister Bonette's haint said the strangest thing. He looked us both straight in the eyes and said with a cold, raspy voice, 'You can have the gold if you tell me where the crown is.' Well, I din't know what in the world he was talking 'bout, so me and Jubal jest took off runnin' with that hand still around Jubal's neck tryin' to strangle him. But finally, Jubal reached up as we were running and ripped those gold necklaces off'en his neck and flung them on the ground. Immediately that bone hand let loose of his neck, reached down, scooped up the gold and flew back to those two haints. Well, me and Jubal din't look back a'tall, we jest took off down that road like mad men.

"But now we *do* know what crown he was talkin' bout," Shadrack said, chuckling deep in his chest.

"Well," Chauncey whispered, "Did ya get away with them jewel rings ya had in your pocket?"

"Yep, I did! We high-tailed it out of there, went down to the French Quarters and sold 'em to one of them underbelly stolen-goods dealers. He din't give us half what they was worth, but it was more'n we had in our pockets, so it was fine with us. After that we high-tailed it back to Missouri."

"So, what did ya want me to come down here for? You said we'd be getting' some gold – are there other graves 'round here with rings and gold chains?"

"No," Shadrack said, leaning closer to Chauncey's face. "It's the crown."

"What crown?" Chauncey said loudly.

"It's the crown Mister Bonette was askin' 'bout. I know where it is, and all we have to do is go get it."

"A gold crown?" Chauncey asked loudly, leaning back again.

Lily, Ophelia and Bob craned their necks trying to hear every word Shadrack had to say.

"Shhh! Don't say it that loud. Sometimes these trees have ears!"

"Ears, ya say? Where? On the sides of their trunks?" Chauncey snorted loudly.

"No, you dummy, sometimes folks be hiding in the woods listening!"

"Ya don't say," Chauncey said, standing up to look around. He spun around and looked boldly all around him. "Well, I ain't seein' nobody!"

"Sometimes they be haints and ghosts, you ignoramus!"

"What?!"

"Yeah," Shadrack whispered, looking anxiously toward the forest. "Haints and ghosts are also huntin' this 'ere par-tic-u-lair gold!"

"Why this one?" Chauncey asked with a frown.

"Hit' has the power to bring 'em back to the livin', and that's what ever' one of 'em wants."

Chauncey sat and stared at Shadrack.

"I ain't believin' it. Ain't no gold has that power. Ain't *nothing* has that power."

"Well," Shadrack shrugged his shoulders. "That's what they're all a'sayin'!"

"So that's what they're doing here," Lily whispered.

"Of course," Bob said with a frown. "They're after the crown."

"What crown?"

Bob looked at Ophelia as if she was from outer space.

"The crown of King Borgward! I just told you before we came through the gate, remember?" He looked as if he thought Ophelia had lost her mind.

"Oh yeah, that's right" Ophelia whispered. "I'm thinking it's a bunch of hogwash."

"Whatever," Bob said, shaking his head in disbelief. "First off, let me say that the only reason I'm telling you this is because Aunt Esabella said the words to you."

"What words?"

"Ophelia, do you *ever* listen to what people say to you? I'm not saying it out loud. It could summon up the same spirit we saw in the garden! Do you really want to see that creature again?"

"Of course I listen!" Ophelia exclaimed. "When I think it's worthwhile, I listen! And yeah, I remember!"

Bob gave her a look of unbelief.

"Well anyway," Lily, "what do we do now?"

Frowning slightly, Bob turned and looked at Lily. "We have to find that crown before anyone else does. If some dead spirits find it, they'll come back to life and live forever. I think that could be a very bad thing. But it's not going to be easy, 'cuz all these skeletons and haints think King Borgward's crown will bring them back to the land of the living. And there's a *whole* lot of haints hunting for it, not to mention living people also! We can't trust anyone! We have to get it back to the rightful owner."

Shaking her head, frowning and wanting to roll her eyes, Lily whispered, "No *crown* is going to give a body back to a haint, a skeleton, or anything! Where did they get such an idea in the first place?"

"I don't know," Bob said, shrugging. "It's been passed down through legend for hundreds of years."

The three of them sat quietly for a few minutes, waiting to see if Shadrack or Chauncey would say any more. They didn't;

they sat quietly, occasionally stoking the fire. Chauncey's leg twitched twice. After some time, Ophelia spoke up.

"You know, every time I see Miss Josephine, I get a strange feeling in my stomach. Something isn't right with her. What do you guys think?"

"There *is* something strange about her," Bob replied. "I've felt it all my life. It's almost like she's not a real flesh and bone person. Plus, I think she knows you have the gift, Lily, and that's why she's always glaring at you."

Goosebumps danced up and down Lily's spine. "Stop saying that, Bob. I don't have *the gift*. Whatever that may be, I don't have it."

"Well, she suspects you," Bob continued. "I'm sure of it - just like she suspects me. There's been more than one time that I've heard her standing quietly at my bedroom door at night, and I would slip out of bed and vanish into the wall where I could watch her without her knowing. One night, not too long ago, I was behind the wall watching, and she silently opened my door and stood there in the pitch-black room, staring at my bed. Thankfully I had pushed a pillow around to look like I was in the bed under the covers! But all of a sudden, she reached into her pocket and pulled out some kind of a charm and shook it over my bed, turned around four times and muttered some sort of gibberish. Then she left the room by going straight through the door, and it looked like she was floating! That's when I figured it out that she didn't want me to be in a room with her when she casts her spells; I'm thinking she knows I have some powers of my own, but she's not sure what they are. She can see ghosts and haints plainer than anyone else, though, I think."

"What did you do?" Ophelia asked, eyes wide open. "And how can you hear her *standing* outside your door?"

"I have strong hearing, almost as keen as a dog. I could hear her breathing."

Lily and Ophelia frowned at Bob.

"Really, Bob?" Lily asked, doubt in her voice.

"Yep, I could," he whispered confidently. "And to answer your question, I slipped back through the wall, stood beside my bed and gave my whole body a good shake, then went to the other side of the bed and did the same. That's how you get rid of a spell if it's been cast upon your bed. Then I climbed in bed and slept like a baby the rest of the night. The next morning at breakfast, Miss Josie gave me the strangest look - not an obviously strange look, but just a slight bit of surprise seemed to flash in her eyes, if you know what I mean. But I acted as if nothing was out of the ordinary and didn't look at her again. Even a slight peek would have given me away, I think. At times, I get chills down my back when she's around. I think she put a spell on my bed that would've done away with me if I slipped into bed and did not know it had been cursed!"

"Probably," Lily whispered.

The three of them turned back to face Shadrack, Chauncey and the fire. Chauncey's boots were so close to the flames that the bottoms were smoking; Shadrack's pant leg had gotten singed by the hot rocks surrounding the firepit.

"Don't this feel mighty fine, my hair-brained friend?" Shadrack asked.

"Indeed, it does, my big-headed, donkey's behind of a friend," Chauncey replied, chuckling. They stretched themselves out on the logs and continued insulting each other lightheartedly. The sound of their laughter echoed amongst the trees that Lily was hiding behind.

Lily heard a loud *CRACK* just as Bob stirred a bit, trying to slowly move away from the tree trunk he had been hiding behind. Terrified, she grabbed him by the shoulder.

"Be *quiet*, you imbicile!" she whispered, trying to stay as quiet as possible.

"It wasn't me!" he responded.

CRACK!

Lily looked back at Ophelia, who had never moved. It wasn't her either.

"We're not alone," Bob whispered under his breath.

CRACK! CRACK!

"It's above us," Ophelia whispered quietly. Lily could hear a tremble in Ophelia's whisper; she was obviously afraid.

The sound of breaking branches, thumps, grunts, and high-pitched yelps filled the treetops all around the fire pit. Even Shadrack and Chauncey had noticed by now and were getting to their feet to see what was closing in on them. Lily could hear her own heartbeat in her ears. Slowly, Lily looked up, afraid of what she might see.

She couldn't tell *what* was coming towards them – it was too dark. The red glow from the fire pit didn't penetrate very deeply into the trees. But at the tops of the trees behind them, branches were bending and breaking, and whatever it was, it was coming right toward them.

Suddenly, two skeletons came crashing from the tops of the trees, bouncing from branch to branch, the sounds of their clacking bones filling the crisp night air. Lily couldn't tell if they dove or fell, but the two skeletons crashed straight into Chauncey and Shadrack's fire pit with a loud *thud*. Loose bones and hot sparks shot up out of the fire in every direction, and deep, gravelly laughter emanated from the pit.

Stunned and terrified, Chauncey and Shadrack stared at the pile of human bones in the middle of the fire. Embers that had been thrown into the night sky were now falling all around them. A deep, hearty voice came from within the fire.

"Well, I guess we best put ourselves back together, mate."

Chauncey, Shadrack, Lily, Bob and Ophelia all stood in dead silence, unsure whether they should run away or laugh.

The fire spun into a small flaming whirlwind as the pile of bones magically moved around, trying to put itself together. Within a few seconds, two human skeletons walked out of the flames, partially charred by the flames. Lily heard that deep chuckle again as the two skeletons shook their bodies like wet dogs, causing loose bones to fall to the ground. Finally, with somewhat of a comical effort, they managed to stand up.

"You sure do clean up nice, chum," one skeleton said to the other. They both laughed heartily with their hands on their hip bones.

"Aye," the other one said with a surprisingly high, squeaky voice. He gave the first skeleton a sharp salute and hopped away from the embers. "I do try, chap!"

They were the strangest skeletons Lily had ever seen! They had bloodshot eyeballs in their sockets, and transparent tongues hung out the sides of their open jaws like panting dogs. Their skulls were cracked in many different places and both had holes above their ears. The skeleton with the high-pitched, squeaky voice was obviously a pirate skeleton with an eye-patch over his left eye and a pirate's scarab hanging though his rib cage. There was a little embellished bag dangling around his neck that rattled with every move he made; Shadrack immediately noticed that it sounded like gold coins clanging around inside it. That skeleton had apparently lost an arm, a leg, and numerous other small bones; he bent down and began scrambling around on his one knee as best he could, trying to sort through the scattered piles of charred bones that were still smoking from the fire.

The second skeleton wore a hip bone on his head like a hat. One of his arms was missing along with one of his foot bones. The hipbone did not, obviously, belong to either of them since they both were currently using their own hipbones.

Eye-Patch popped his jawbone into place and snapped his neck bones twice to get his jaw adjusted rightly. Looking at his friend, he pointed with his one arm and shouted, "Aye! That's my arm and my hand, mate!"

"No, no, it's not! It's mine - look at the long fingers!" Hip-Hat shouted back, waving the hand vigorously as one of his teeth flew out and landed on top of Shadrack's pot-bellied stomach.

"No, it's mine! Look at your arms - you already have a left and a right."

"Ah... So I do, mate. So I do! Pardon me."

"No problem, mate," Eye-Patch muttered. "Would ya' toss me that leg bone next to ya? That's mine too."

"It's called a femur, you know," Hip-Hat said, laughing. "You should know that, you old bag o'bones!"

"Okay, whatever mate, just gimme my leg!"

"How about I trade you for that calcaneus your sorry behind is sitting on? I do believe that one is mine."

"That what?"

"That foot bone, you dim-wit! It's called a calcaneus."

"Well, well, professor," Eye-Patch said with a chuckle, "let me try it on and take a gander - maybe your feet can run faster than mine!" He snapped off his right foot, jammed Hip-Hat's bone onto his ankle, lifted it up and took a good, long look at it.

"Naw," Eye-Patch said, "you can have it back. It ain't the right size. And if we find King Borgward's crown, I ain't wanting to have my feet different sizes!" He casually tossed the foot bone and it landed right next to Hip-Hat's ankle.

Just as Hip-Hat was clicking his foot back on, Chauncey jumped up to his feet. "Hey! Get out of here, you heathen skeletons! You can't find the crown because you ain't smart enough! And skeletons are not allowed - remember the code? So leave on out and stop your searchin'!"

"Hang the code, mate," Eye-Patch yelled back at Chauncey, not even looking at him. "We're finding it whether you like it or not. The code makes no difference to us! Ain't that right, Arch?"

"That's right, mate," Hip-Hat called out, still shuffling through the pile of bones, also not caring to look at Chauncey.

Chauncey was obviously frustrated. Lily could see his eyes bugging out all the way from her hiding spot in the trees. "I know *you*," he said, his anger rising as he walked towards Hip-Hat, shaking his finger. "Yes, indeed, I know you! You're that bloke who pushed me into the muddy road in Sydney and stole my coin pouch! You're Nevil Bindi from the outback of Australia – and you still have my coin pouch, you thieving scoundrel! I demand that you release it to me immediately!"

Jumping back with a loud yelp, Nevil's single eye popped out of its socket and hung down on his cheek by a cord. The skeleton tenderly held his eye in his one hand and moved it around so he could see Chauncey, then shoved it back into its socket with a loud *pop!* and whipped his arm into the air like a man being arrested. Nevil screamed, his long, transparent tongue flapping in the air, startling Chauncey and making him jump back. Reaching up, Nevil slapped his eyeball again just to make sure it stayed put, flung his bones around and took off down the cobblestone pathway.

Lily stifled her laughter. She couldn't help but smile as she watched Nevil run down the path, still screaming at the top of his lungs, his arm whipping around in circles high above his head like a whirligig. Long-legged Chauncey took off after him, running faster than Lily would have believed he could, if she hadn't seen it herself.

"Come here, you thieving scoundrel!" Chauncey shrieked. "I'm gonna catch you and rip you bone from bone!"

Everyone else stood and stared at Nevil and Chauncey as they ran off.

"Good riddance," Archie muttered. Snorting, he bent down again and continued gathering loose bones. Picking up three ribs, he held them up and stared at them in the light of the fire for a moment before raising his left arm and sticking them into his armpit, one by one. They seemed to click into place. He gave his arm a shake and the three ribs clanked against each other like wind chimes blowing in a breeze. Smiling, Archie hopped around in a circle, doing a short little dance. He held his left arm straight out from his body and used his other arm to create a tune by clanking his loose ribs.

After his quick jig, he bent down and began rustling around in the dirt again. He picked up a leg bone and examined it closely. Reaching up and pulling the hip bone off his head, he put this new leg bone into his skull by shoving it hard enough to make a small hole, then put the hip bone back on his head, sliding the leg bone through the hole in the hip bone. The leg bone stuck up through the hip bone like a horn growing out of his skull. Imagining what he must look like, he snorted and chuckled, he got down on his hands and knees and again dug through the grass looking for more bones. Lily noticed that by this time, both Archie and Nevil had both their legs. She wondered whose leg was now being worn as a hat.

Jerking his body straight up into a sitting position, the skeleton stuck his thumb into his mouth like a little child and leaned forward a bit, peering intently into the forest. Shadrack too was sitting in a stunned stupor, a look of pure fright covering his face as he stared into the trees.

"This isn't good," Bob muttered under his breath, pulling Lily and Ophelia further down into the tall grass. "It's not good a'tall when a *skeleton* gets alarmed."

Sucking loudly on his thumb bone as if it were covered with molasses, Archie leaned his body to one side, paused and stared into the woods, then leaned the other way to look again. Slowly he turned his head towards the three of them, took his thumb out of his mouth and pointed aggressively at the trees he had been staring at. Immediately putting his thumb in his mouth again, he cautiously stood to his feet, took one step back, and then another. He looked again in their direction, pointed forcefully once more, then waved his hand at them dismissively. Suddenly, Archie jumped almost three feet into the air, shrieking loudly enough to shatter their eardrums as he dove, his transparent red tongue flapping in the wind, straight into the giant elm tree where the three of them were huddled.

Archie's shriek woke Shadrack from his frightened trance; he gave his round body a shake and jumped higher than anyone Lily had ever seen anyone jump. In a flash, he was gone down the pathway towards the cemetery gate.

Bob, Lily and Ophelia huddled on the wet ground, frantically doing their best to silently peer through the brush to see what could have possibly scared Archie and Shadrack so badly. Lily saw her first.

Half hidden behind a large elm tree stood Miss Josephine herself. Her long, black hair was no longer in a tight bun at the nape of her neck; it was now blowing wildly around her head like she was standing in a strong wind. Her black eyes were flashing sparks in the dusky, dark forest and her face was more menacing than before.

Feeling a brush against her elbow, Lily glanced at Bob just in time to see him melt quietly into the elm tree. Without warning, his two arms shot out from the tree and snatched both her and Ophelia inside!

Blinking rapidly, Lily looked at her new surroundings. The giant elm tree was hollow inside. As her eyes adjusted, she saw Bob, but he wasn't alone! Archie was sitting right next to him, sucking on his thumb.

The inside of the tree seemed much bigger than the outside. Wet moss covered the interior walls, and tiny baby branches covered every inch of the trunk's interior. The odor of mold and rotting foliage filled Lily's senses.

Spellbound with what had just happened, Ophelia began to speak quietly. "What – what did you just do, Bob?" She looked over at Lily. "Lily, I feel rather faint."

"Don't faint, Ophelia!" Lily hissed loudly.

"Okay," she answered, her face turning white as her eyes began rolling to the back of her head.

"Don't!" Lily hissed louder.

Ophelia's eyes rolled back into place and her face regained its pink hue.

"What was that about?" Bob whispered, staring at Ophelia.

"Nothing. None of your business," Ophelia said, staring at Bob furiously. Saying nothing in return, Bob stared at Ophelia as if *she* were the strange one.

"What in the heck was that, Bob?" Lily demanded, glaring angrily.

"I'll tell you later. Just look at the sides of the tree and we can watch."

"Okay," Lily whispered, shaking her head. She had come to realize nothing was normal when they were around Bob.

"What now? All I see is wood."

"Wait," Bob replied.

A mass of small branches in front of them began wiggling, slithering like little snakes. After a moment, they parted; suddenly there was an opening as the wood seemed to thin into something like glass. It was like a window had appeared all by itself. However, it also seemed to shine outwardly; Lily noticed a new light on the entire forest. She could see the pile of ashes that Archie and Nevil had crashed into, she could see the path leading back to the gate, and there in plain sight, at the edge of the forest, stood Miss Josephine.

Something cold and as rough as sandpaper brushed against Lily's face. Archie's skull had pushed tightly between her and Bob's faces as it too peered into the lit forest. He sheepishly rolled his bloodshot eyeballs towards Lily before darting them back outside. Lily did not look at him, but she could feel his eyes darting back to look at her again.

Tap, tap, tap. The skeleton's rough, boney finger tapped on the side of Lily's nose.

"What?" Lily whispered sharply, vigorously rubbing the side of her nose.

Holding his fist up to his face, again he jabbed his finger back and forth, but now towards a different area of the forest. Lily frowned at him, then turned her head to look. Her jaw dropped.

There in full light stood the ghost of Annabelle Bloome, walking with the flesh-and-bones body of Mr. Kulicki! Mr. Kulicki was snapping his fingers loudly and shaking his fist in the direction of Miss Josephine.

"Kerfuffle, kerfuffle, kerfuffle!" Mr. Kulicki's voice boomed and echoed throughout the entire cemetery.

Whirling around with a fuming snarl, Miss Josephine vanished into the dusty night, her wild hair spinning around her face as her long, black cloak swooped violently around her body. Lily could still hear the echoes of her sneer bouncing from tree to tree in the thick woods around the forest. After a moment, peace seemed to settle into the cemetery grounds. Mister Kulicki and Miss Annabelle's apparition calmly strolled along the path leading back to the mansion.

Archie, Bob, and the girls stood silently inside the tree, stunned, for what seemed like an eternity. until Lily spoke up.

"So, Bob," she whispered, "how do we get out of here?" Ophelia was impressed at how Lily was totally ignoring the presence of a real skeleton standing beside her.

Archie had been trying, not so discreetly, to untie the ribbon Lily had tied round her long braid. When Lily asked about a way out, he looked her in the eyes, snapped his boney jaws a couple times and grabbed her arm with his cold, boney hand.

CRACK!

With a sound similar to the snap of a breaking branch, Archie had somehow whipped Lily out of that tree the same way that Bob had put them into it. Not a moment later, Bob and Ophelia followed, Bob firmly gripping Ophelia's arm.

"Well," Lily whispered, "I guess that answered my question."

Lily looked around cautiously. The cemetery was quiet, but the peace they had felt after Miss Josephine left was slowly starting to fade. An owl called loudly above them, making Ophelia gasp quietly. Leaves fluttered and rustled in the balmy breeze, which had warmed a little from earlier. Lily heard the quiet roll of distant thunder, along with the lonesome sound of a train's whistle, echoing across the flat lands on its way down to New Orleans.

"We might as well go back," Bob whispered uneasily. "I think it's going to storm, and for some reason when the apparitions and phantoms roam the woods, the storms become violent."

Once again, Archie tugged on the ribbon in Lily's hair. Reaching back, Lily jerked her braid out of the skeleton's hands and untied her ribbon.

"Here," She said as she secured her ribbon around his wrist, "you can have it." She looked him square in the eye. "Now, don't lose it, it's my favorite."

"Okay," the skeleton replied in a squeaky, bone-against-bone voice.

"What is wrong with me? I'm talking to a skeleton as if it's a normal thing," Lily muttered to herself.

Turning quickly, Lily, Ophelia and Bob walked silently through the grass of the cemetery grounds towards the cobblestone path; their eyes darted from tree to tree in nervous anticipation.

Clink-clank.

Clink-clank.

The sound came from directly behind them; Archie's bones clanked as he walked. The three stopped and turned around. When they looked at Archie, who was following close behind Lily, he also stopped and looked around, as if it was not him they were looking at. After an awkward pause, he reached up and scratched his skull with his right hand, then broke the thumb off his left hand and stuck it in his mouth before motioning them to look at a headstone next to Bob. There, in bold letters, the engraving on the headstone read:

Here lies the body of
Archie Bald Crumb
Shot by his wife for sucking his thumb.
Born Feb 1, 1602 – Died Oct 1, 1699

Staring at the headstone, then back at Archie, the three of them waited for him to say something. The silence was awkward.

"How-do, Mr. Crumb?" Bob asked politely.

"How-do?" Lily and Ophelia chimed.

The skeleton stood beside his own grave with his head hanging low. Then, whipping his arm into the air, Archie bent his hand at the wrist and dramatically pointed his finger towards the headstone next to his, which read:

Here lies the body of
Anthelia Crumb
Shot old Archie for sucking his thumb
Then fell over dead when she guzzled his rum
Born March 15, 1617 – Died Oct 1, 1699

The quiet, awkward tension only increased. Then, suddenly, the silence was broken.

Click CLACK.

Click click click CLACK.

Archie's jaw snapped up and down; his shoulders and ribs shook. He was laughing, silently at first, then developing into an eerie, deep chuckle emanating from his empty rib cage. Staring, jaw dropped, Lily was sure she could make out a fleeting smirk on his boney face.

"Serves her right," he said in his gravelly voice. He stopped laughing, and Lily thought she saw his forehead bone twist into a scowl. "She was a mean one. She cast spells on me so she could watch me lap up water like a dog from the mud holes in the road!"

Lily, Ophelia and Bob listened intently, watching Archie closely.

"I told her many a time, 'Don't touch my jug-o-rum', but would she listen to me? Nope! So, she got what she deserved!"

Without another second's hesitation, Archie dove skull-first into his grave, and – *SNAP* – he was gone, leaving only his broken-off thumb lying wiggling on the ground. Both the girls gasped, startled by his quick movements. Before they had even calmed down, Archie's boney hand burst up from his grave, snatched his thumb bone and popped back down into the earth. Not one second later, the three of them could hear him slurping on his thumb; it sounded just like kids slurping on a chunk of ice in the hot summertime.

Mesmerized, they stood staring at the two headstones, wondering if Archie was going to come back up. After a brief moment of silence, the three of them fell to the ground in uncontrollable laughter.

"Well," Bob said breathlessly, "that was strange!"

Thunder rolled a little louder as the girls regained their composure.

"Let's get out of here," Bob said, still smiling. "The storm's a'comin'".

4

The Funeral

It was the day of Annabelle's funeral, and Lily was feeling miserable and unhappy Earlier that morning, well before dawn, Lily had awakened to the loud cries of Mr. Kulicki's crows as they flew off their usual stone wall perch behind the house and vanished into the dark sky without a trace. She rolled over and fell asleep again quickly, resting soundly until the sun woke her up.

Once full morning had come and Vicksburg had stirred itself together for the funeral, Annabelle's coffin was pulled slowly to St. John's cathedral in a hearse drawn by four big, high-stepping stallions with glistening black coats, draped in black mourning blankets. The driver, sitting stately atop the slow-moving hearse with perfectly straight posture, was also clothed entirely in black; Lily had noticed his tall, satin, stove-pipe hat glistening in the sunshine – as well as his knee-high boots. Walking behind the hearse in dismal silence was Ophelia, Bob and the rest of the family, followed by other citizens of Vicksburg, Lily could not hear a single bird singing. It was unusual for this time of day.

The procession, every individual dressed in black, wound its way through the meandering, cobblestone streets with only the creaking sound of the hearse and the echo of horse's hooves striking the cobblestones, which echoed eerily throughout the silent city. The sound seemed to touch Lily's soul. The procession included not only Annalise's family, but also neighbors and people from poor families living in shanties along the water; everyone walked with heads bent in respect. Lily remembered how Annabelle had made a habit of befriending people of every neighborhood, even bringing food, clothing, and occasional medical help to anyone who had a need.

The hearse slowly made its way to St. John's cathedral, which sat at the edge of the Mississippi riverbank. Lily heard the waves slapping the river bank; it seemed much louder than normal. She turned and watched the river as she and the rest of the procession approached the cathedral. Rolling and churning violently, the water seemed agitated. White caps rose high above its surface as it sped past the church, and savage waves beat against the shoreline like hands slapping angrily at flies.

Being the oldest church along the Mississippi, the majestic Cathedral had two elaborate steeples above the entrance doors that soared fifty feet into the sky. Below the steeples, the two intricately carved, wooden double doors were wide enough for a horse drawn carriage to pass through. Rays of sunlight sparkled brightly on the steps leading up to the doors.

Breaking the silence, the lonesome song of mourning doves echoed sporadically up from the riverbank. Their song seemed to give nature permission to speak. Lily heard Otto's old hound Henry whining softly as he sat beside the cathedral door. Evidently the old hound had traveled to the church before sunrise to claim his spot.

Lily looked around the crowded cobblestone streets. She was near the front of the procession, and although she knew it would not be proper to turn and stare at those walking behind them, she was curious as to where Miss Josephine might be. Lily had not seen her yet this morning. She'd seen the others - Mr. Kulicki, Bob, Mr. Porter, Mrs. Esabella, and Mr. Pat with some of his family too.

"Suspicious", Lily thought.

Drawing up to St John's entrance, the hearse stopped just outside the doors. Six elegantly dressed men rolled Mrs. Annabelle's coffin into the church as the crowd filed slowly into the somber sanctuary. The old hound Henry walked sadly behind the pallbearers, then took his stand beside the coffin. Lily remembered that Henry had spent more time with Annabelle than with anyone else.

The priests directed everyone to take a seat. Lily, Ophelia and Bob sat in the second row, next to the middle aisle. The organist began playing softly. Standing solemnly behind the podium was a hunched-over, old priest named Father Fitz; he was no longer the keeper of the parish, but Otto had asked if he would officiate Mrs. Annabelle's funeral since he had been their priest for many years.

After all the mourners were seated, the kind, old priest adjusted his biretta, pushed his cockeyed glasses up onto his long, thin nose, and raised his grizzled, shaking hand, signaling the pallbearers to open the coffin so everyone could view Mrs. Annabelle's body.

A soft murmur swept across the church as folks stood to their feet to see Mrs. Annabelle's body. Surrounded by flowers, she looked like a porcelain figure. Never in a million years would most folks had believed Mrs. Annabelle had been a mischief-maker.

Raising both his hands, Father Fitz made the motion for all to be seated, but the large crowd completely ignored him. The murmur of shuffling feet and hushed voices continued. Father Fitz tried again, unsuccessfully. Finally, the old priest cleared his throat.

"SIT DOWN!" He yelled as loud as he could. He flapped his arms up and down so the crowd would take a hint. Red-faced with embarrassment, the crowd eventually sat down and bowed their heads.

As if he hadn't ever raised his voice, Father Fitz bowed his head and began his monotone prayer. Lily did not bow her head, but continued to gaze at Mrs. Annabelle's body. Suddenly, her spirit sat straight up in the coffin, turned her head towards Lily, waved and smiled from ear to ear. She swung her legs over the edge of the coffin, gave herself a little jumping scoot, and sat on her own body's flesh-and-bone legs. The spirit was swinging her ghostly legs back and forth outside the coffin, as if nothing was unusual about what was happening. She looked around the room at the large crowd and waved, almost as if it was expected of her!

Lily blinked a few times and shook her head trying to clear her eyes of the apparition. When she opened her eyes, Mrs. Annabelle was making eye contact with Lily, grinning broadly. Poking Ophelia in the side, Lily turned and looked at her friend. Ophelia was as white as a ghost herself, and sweat was running down the sides of her face. Lily instinctively grabbed Ophelia's hand, leaned in close and whispered in the most demanding tone she could manage without being noticed.

"Don't you faint, Ophelia! Don't!"

Ophelia swallowed hard and nodded. She held Lily's hand so hard it hurt.

"Let go! You're hurting my hand!" Lily hissed quietly.

"I can't or I will fall over in a faint!"

"No, you will not! Don't you even think about it!" Lily tried squeezing Ophelia's hand even harder than Ophelia was squeezing hers. Ophelia eased up a bit, and the blood flowed back into Lily's fingers.

The girls looked back at the coffin. Mrs. Annabelle's spirit waved again, smiled, and put her finger to her lips, telling them to be quiet.

Ophelia felt Bob poke her in her side. She turned to look at him, and he was grinning from ear to ear. He put his finger to his mouth, telling her to be quiet. Ophelia turned and poked Lily in the side, who turned to see Bob smiling broadly and waving at Annabelle. Lily looked back at Annabelle, who was waving back at Bob. Henry, the old hound, got up from his position at the head of her coffin and, wagging his tail, walked over to where her legs were dangling and sat on his haunches. She reached down and ruffled his hair, making him whine with contentment. Lily was anxious, wondering if anyone else in the cathedral could see what was happening. Surely someone could at least see the dog's hair moving! Glancing around the room, no one seemed to have noticed. Lily didn't see the old gentleman standing by the back door of the crowded cathedral, though.

"Good Lord Almighty," the man exclaimed loudly, interrupting Father Fitz' monotonous prayers, "I – I – I see 'ah haint a'floatin' above 'er coffin!" With a look of utter terror on his face, he lifted his arm and pointed at Annabelle's coffin. The crowd didn't know whether to turn around and see who was talking, or to look at the coffin. Nervous excitement quickly filled the room.

"What's he talking about?" a child asked.

"I don't see anything," another woman said, rolling her eyes.

Apparently, almost nobody could see Annabelle's ghost. Lily was surprised. She didn't know if she should feel anxious, or if she should be laughing.

THUD.

The old gentleman collapsed on the floor. At that point, everyone turned to look at the man. Some men jumped up to get a better look and see if he needed help. At this point, Lily, Bob and Ophelia couldn't help but laugh a little.

Father Fitz seemed stunned for a minute, but came-to and tried to restore order to the room.

"Brother Bartholomew, Brother Phillip, please help dear Mr. Pettibone outside for some fresh air. I believe he is overcome with grief," Father Fitz said softly.

Looking back to the front, Lily watched as Mrs. Annabelle's spirit swooped to the back of the chapel and stood beside Mr. Pettibone, who was by now standing - with the help of Brother Bartholomew and Brother Phillip. She put her arm around Mr. Pettibone and whispered in his ear. Suddenly, Mr. Pettibone pulled away from the two brothers and told them sternly that he was fine, insisting he stay in the chapel. After a moment of hesitation, they agreed and helped him to a seat that a nearby young man volunteered to give up.

By the time Mr. Pettibone was seated, Mrs. Annabelle was already back sitting on her own coffin. Father Fitz sighed deeply and motioned for everyone to take their seats. Once again, he bowed his head and continued his prayer. Lily continued to look straight ahead.

Strangely enough, when Father Fitz bowed his head, Lily caught him staring straight at Mrs. Annabelle, frowning. He shook his head subtly, and in a very brief pause of his prayer, he silently mouthed the word "No". Immediately, Mrs. Annabelle flopped her spirit down on top of her physical body, her spirit sitting on her body's chest with her ghostly legs dangling off the side of the coffin. Playfully but calmly, she swung her ghostly legs back and forth again, listening to Father Fitz' prayer. As soon as his prayer ended, the old priest glanced down at her again and nodded his head as if to say that he appreciated her cooperation; he cleared his throat and began sharing a sermon in Latin.

His voice seemed to drone on and on. Bored and unable to understand Latin, Lily gazed at Mrs. Annabelle's apparition, who also seemed barely able to sit still. After a few minutes, the ghost yawned widely, closed her eyes, leaned her head back against the coffin lid and began to snore - loudly.

The congregation craned their heads around to see the rude individual who would snore at a funeral. Lily, Ophelia and Bob stifled laughter under their breath, not showing a hint of emotion externally. Father Fitz stopped speaking, looked down at the coffin, and a gentle, kind voice, said, "That is quite enough, my dear. Please behave yourself during this time of sorrow."

Mrs. Annabelle's spirit jumped straight up to her feet, still standing on her body's stomach. Snapping her feet together and looking him in the eye, she offered a military salute, then dove head-first back into her body. The old priest chuckled under his breath. Lily noticed the smallest little grin on his wise, furrowed face as he looked down at his notes and continued his homily.

Everyone in the building was staring at Lily and Ophelia, assuming one of them were the guilty culprit the father had reprimanded. Somehow, Father Fitz seemed to realize this. Pausing and looking up from his papers, Father Fitz spoke up. "T'was not the lasses in the second row, my fellow Vicksburgians. Pay no attention to my prior comment."

Mouth open in surprise, Lily stared at Father Fitz; he glanced at her again and gave her a quick, subtle wink before returning to his homily. Lily continued to stare open-mouthed at him. A moment later, he paused briefly between two Latin sentences and lowered his voice, not looking up from his notes.

"Aye, lass, I too can see her," he said, immediately rolling into his next sentence as if this short English phrase was written into the homily.

Snickering, Ophelia poked Lily in the side with her elbow and motioned for Lily to look at the coffin. Mrs. Annabelle's ghostly hand was slowly and playfully inching its fingers out of the coffin, until her whole arm was exposed, then her shoulders and head; a goofy grin spread from one side of her face to the other. Her whole spirit slithered right out of the coffin like an eel, but so slowly it reminded Lily of a blob of fog floating down a dark road. Eventually, she popped up to her feet and began twirling around in circles with her ghostly dress flowing out behind her. It seemed that Lily, Ophelia and Bob were the only ones who could see her. Up and down the church aisles she waltzed, smiling with her arms spread wide. As she passed her sister Esabella - who was seated in the front row - she flicked her hat off her head. It landed in a giant pot of flowers sitting beside the pew. Esabella reached into the flower pot with a slight grin, shaking her head. As if nothing had happened, she reached over, removed her hat from the pot and put it back on her head.

Lily was curious if old Mr. Pettibone could still see Mrs. Annalise. She turned around as discreetly as she could to look. Sure enough, he was on his feet, gawking at Mrs. Annabelle with his mouth hanging open and his eyes bugged out like a bull frog.

"Please close the door, Brother Bartholomew," Father Fitz asked calmly with a smile on his face. "There seems to be quite a breeze coming in from the outside." Lily got the feeling he was enjoying Mrs. Annabelle's last happy dance. He looked back down at his papers.

"The breeze has no idea how disrespectful it is being," he said quietly.

Then Lily's heart sank.

Behind Father Fitz at the pulpit, half-hidden by the large crucifix at the far side of the podium, stood Miss Josephine. Lily's heart began pounding loudly in her chest as she felt the surge of adrenaline fill her body and Mrs. Annabelle must have spotted Miss Josephine at the same time as Lily. She immediately took a flying leap off the red roses she was perched upon and dove into her body.

THUD, CLICK.

Mrs. Annabelle herself loudly closed and locked the lid on her own coffin. A terribly eerie silence immediately descended upon the crowd. Knowing full-well the slight breeze was not strong enough to close the coffin, everyone was holding their breath. Lily could feel the anxiety in the air as darkness started covering the stained-glass windows. Within seconds, the interior of the high ceiling cathedral had become black as midnight.

"Brother Bartholomew," Father Fitz said in a controlled whisper, "please have Brother Phillip help you light the lanterns along the walls."

With shaking hands, the two men began lighting the lanterns hanging on each wall of the cathedral with the torches in their hands. Lily watched as Brother Phillip tried lighting the last lantern, then again, then again for a third time. His hands were shaking too much for the flame to catch. He gave up and briskly walked back to his seat.

Softly, Father Fitz began to sing an old hymn from long ago and the crowd quickly fueled the chorus with voices as they joined Father Fritz's ancient, wavering voice.

The flickering lanterns brightened as the flames grabbed hold of the wicks. Rays of light flickered and grew, pushing against the darkness. The congregation continued to sing even louder. Father Fitz stopped singing altogether as the congregation continued.

Squinting her eyes, Lily looked up at the crucifix. Miss Josephine was no longer behind it. Lily's eyes scrambled to find Miss Josephine; she knew she would not leave that easily. The light from the torches continued to grow brighter. Continuing to look around the room, Lily found her. Although she was hard to see, there she was, standing directly behind Father Fitz. Her entire form was black and shadowy, like she was enveloped in a black shroud of death. Father Fitz was standing completely straight, his eyes fastened, to the entrance to the church. He looked to be taller than he had a few minutes before. His right hand grasped the large, silver cross hanging around his neck.

Miss Josephine raised her arm. It looked like she was going to strike out at Father Fitz.

"FATHER!" Lily yelled.

POOF.

The entire cathedral was immediately engulfed in complete darkness. Lily couldn't see a thing – not even her hand in front of her face. Lily continued to yell.

"FATHER! WATCH OUT! THERE'S -"

Before she could get his attention, Father Fitz had already whirled himself around to stand face-to-face with Miss Josephine, holding the cross to her face and staring her in the eyes. A dramatic flash of white and yellow fire burst from the cross, lighting up the entire cathedral before vanishing in a matter of seconds. With a loud, terrible, blood-curdling scream, the black clad creature flew into the air then flew like lightning out the door of the cathedral – which, seconds earlier, Brother Bartholomew had scrambled to open as if he knew what was about to happen. Immediately, the lanterns were lit again, and the congregation could see.

Sitting in stunned silence, everyone stared at Father Fitz, waiting for an explanation as to what just took place. Golden rays of sunshine once again streamed through the stained-glass windows; after a few seconds of silence, Lily could hear birds singing outside.

But Father Fitz's eyes were still focused on the open door. He blinked a few times, swallowed hard, and bowed his head as if in prayer.

"The good Lord giveth," he said, "and the good Lord taketh away."

5

A Cry in the distance

Mr. Kulicki had left the funeral early to retrieve the large, Brougham carriage so Annabelle's family could ride from the cathedral to the cemetery in comfort. Mr. Kulicki was not only their butler; he was also the coachman, the watchman and the keeper of the massive family gardens, which included the cemetery.

The Bloome family's large, shiny, black Brougham carriage ambled through the streets in somber silence. It trailed behind the cathedral's carriage, which was carrying Father Fitz, Brother Bartholomew and Brother Phillip. The procession was led by the horse-drawn hearse, which held Mrs. Annabelle's coffin. The people of Vicksburg stood respectfully with hat in hand until the procession passed by. Most of the citizens of Vicksburg did not attend this smaller event - gravesite services were a private affair for family and close friends only.

Lily listened to the *clip-clop* of horse's hooves on cobblestone as the carriages reached the gate of the private cemetery. The family stepped solemnly from the Brougham and walked to the grave, waiting for Annabelle's coffin to be carried to its site. When all was in proper order, Father Fitz began his graveside speech. Lily could hear sadness in his ancient voice as he spoke of all the good Annabelle Bloome had done for his congregation. Not once did he hint of all the mischief Mrs. Annabelle has gotten into, but only the joy she gave to others.

"Lord on high, receive her soul into your arms," he asked humbly. "Give her peace."

Lily watched as sorrow distorted the old man's weathered face. Tears streamed down his wrinkled cheeks and his raspy voice wavered.

"She was one of the best, dear family. One of the best."

Taking a couple steps back, Father Fitz quoted a solemn scripture from the Bible, and the coffin was lowered into the ground. Mr. Kulicki motioned for the grave diggers to fill in the open spot.

Looking out across the cemetery, Lily's took in the beautiful, flowering garden as she listened to the sound of shovelfuls of dirt falling onto Mrs. Annabelle's coffin.

Thud.

Thud.

An almost stifling heaviness weighed on her chest as her mind flew back to the happy days she had spent with Mrs. Annabelle.

Thud.

Mrs. Annabelle had been strange even in the eyes of five-year-old Lily. During their first meeting, Lily knew she was different from any other woman she had met - she had a special air about her.

Thud.

Thud.

Thud.

As she continued to reminisce, a very foreign sound, probably the strangest she had ever heard, disrupted her thoughts. It sounded as if a giant cat was purring far off in the distance. It almost sounded like a growl, but it was soft, and sorrowful. It grew louder, echoing across the landscape, far past the village of Vicksburg. It was somewhat similar to the lonesome call of the river loon, if a loon was bigger and could purr.

Not one person in the small group said a word, but everyone had their eyes fixed on the distant spot where it seemed to be coming from - approximately two miles to the north, in the hill country. As they looked, a light flashed in the hills as if someone was holding a mirror up to the sky.

"It's the dragon," Bob whispered quietly, his voice trembling with excitement. He spoke quietly so only Lily could hear him. "He's mourning Aunt Anna B's death. I can feel it in my bones."

This was not the kind of thing Lily wanted to hear right now.

"Bob," she whispered sternly, "there are no such things as dragons. Where did you hear of such malarkey?"

"From Aunt Anna B herself! Didn't she ever tell you the story of meeting the dragon over on Dragon's Lair Hills?"

"No."

"Well, she told me," he replied matter-of-factly as he turned his head away.

Ophelia looked at Bob as if he had gone stark-raving crazy. Once again, the loud, muffled purr swept across the cemetery. The adults began murmuring and shuffling around a bit. Father Fitz quickly spoke the closing words of the service, then he and the Brothers scrambled into their carriage to leave.

Mr. Kulicki hastily ushered the family members into the Brougham. No one hesitated.

The ride back to the mansion passed in total silence. Everyone kept their faces turned toward the hills, half expecting to see something appear in the distance. As they drew near the carriage house, the sound stopped.

Immediately Otto, Mr. Pat, Mr. Porter and the other adults hurried into the house as Mr. Kulicki's crows perched on the stone wall. Bob, Lily and Ophelia jumped over the edge of the carriage and raced into the house, following the adults.

They had hardly made it inside when the sad, mournful sound returned, causing the three of them to freeze in their tracks, looking at each other with eyes wide.

"Why is it purring again?" Lily whispered very quietly, as if talking too loudly would conjure up the creature right there in the kitchen. She turned to look outside.

"I don't know," Bob muttered softly, looking out a window. He stood motionless, staring outside.

"Hey," he said squeakily, "look!" He was pointing his finger towards the hills.

Jumping to the window, Lily and Ophelia pushed in close to Bob so all three of them could have a good view. A dark cloud slowly covered the distant hills, and eerily silent lightning flashed from the cloud in jagged streaks.

"What is happening?" Ophelia whispered, clearly anxious and frightened.

No one answered her.

Lily saw it first. Looking toward the dragon's mountain, it alone was covered in darkness as if this mountain was where the birth of darkness began be it good or bad, then up from the strange mountain rose a dragon so large it seemed to

100

overshadow the entire mountains themselves. Its body was ice-blue, and even though it was miles away, somehow Lily could see its huge red-hot eyes glowing as if on fire. Opening its enormous mouth, the beast bellowed out the most sorrowful, soul-wrenching sound known to mankind. Its vast, feathered wings rose high above its head and its body quivered and shook like it was sobbing. Lily wasn't sure if she should feel bad for this beast or run away in terror. Suddenly its massive barbed tail rose high above its head then snapped sharply against the sky, sending a loud *CRACK* shooting across the delta. The sky above the mountain then shattered like a broken window and a chorus of tinkling and pinging like that of a thousand broken windows echoed and rebounded across the land as the great dragon, with a howl of anguish, slipped through the open window of the night sky and vanished, leaving behind the tinkling sounds of shattered crystal falling to earth.

"Hey," someone whispered behind them. The three jumped around, scared out of their minds.

Katie, Mr. Pat's daughter, was right behind them.

"Can you all come help me serve cakes and brandy? Then we can all go sit in the parlor and listen to what everyone is saying."

Katie gently touched Lily and Ophelia on the shoulders and said in a kind voice, "Please, for your own sake and for that of others, let's not mention to anyone else what we just witnessed."

The three of them stared at her for a bit and silently nodded in unison. They were so relieved that Katie was not Miss Josephine reappearing that they didn't question her request at all. With a sigh of relief, they smiled and followed her into the kitchen where she had already started a fire in the big wrought-iron stove. It was already warm in this room, and Katie had made warm tea cakes; brandy was steaming from the stove.

The three of them followed her silently into the parlor, carrying the heavy-laden trays full of miniature cakes and sandwiches. When Brother Bartholomew and Brother Phillip saw the girls, they jumped up and helped place the food and beverages on the side table. Otto was talking with Father Fitz quietly. Mr. Kulicki walked in with an armful of cut flowers from the cathedral; he placed them around the room in cut-glass vases.

"Mr. Kulicki," Otto said gently to his butler, "come, have a seat, my good fellow. You are more than a butler to this family; you are one of our own. I have grown to love you as if you are my own blood brother, just as I know both Annabelle and Esabella have done."

Mr. Kulicki's wrinkled, weathered face eased into a broad smile and his eyes sparkled with glistening tears as he took a seat next to Otto at the small table. Otto poured him a sniffer of brandy.

Placing one fist under his chin and the other on his waist, Otto looked at his loyal butler with an expression of bewilderment.

"My dear friend," Otto spoke in a soft, gentle voice, "What, pray tell, is going on here in our home? I have never, for the life of me, seen anything like Miss Josephine at St John's today."

Mr. Kulicki bent his head and sighed.

"Mr. Otto"

"Please," Otto said kindly, "please call me Otto."

"Otto," Mr. Kulicki continued, smiling, "Josephine is a bad one. I felt it when first she came into our home, but I wasn't sure, so I could not point a finger at her nor accuse her of any wrong doings."

The room became as quiet as a tomb as everyone waited for him to continue. Lily, Ophelia and Bob had taken seats on the large, marble hearth. They all leaned in, not wanting to miss a single word.

"I am sorry, my dear children," he said calmly. "I wish I had known sooner, but I did not. It wasn't until you sent me on that business trip to New Orleans did I learn who she really was – or is. When I returned, Mrs. Annabelle had vanished and I could not bring myself to lay more heartache on you. I truly did not realize how bad it was and how involved *she* was in the entire scenario, or I would have done so. But I kept a close eye on her and stopped her from doing many bad deeds."

He cleared his throat before he continued; he appeared quite nervous. The eyes of the whole room were transfixed on him.

"You see, this is the story I gleaned from my acquaintances in Vacherie, Louisiana," he said, pausing to clear his throat a second time. Lily heard thunder rolling in the distance.

"Miss Josephine's real name is Dauphine Josephina Marie Ladeaux. She was born in the French Quarter of New Orleans in the 1750's. She grew up on a sugar cane plantation in Vacherie, some fifty miles or so outside of New Orleans. Her mother had become involved in the voodoo of the French Quarters, and eventually left her husband, so he had to raise eighteen children by himself. Her father was a poor farmer who was heavily indebted to some wealthy plantation owners, and he gave himself and his children to the owners to cut the cane and try to pay off his debts. When Dauphine reached the age of sixteen, she ran away from her father's ramshackle home and met up with her mother in New Orleans where she too became involved in practicing the voodoo.

"Voodoo is not a thing to dabble in, my dear folks - not a good thing at all. It is a thing of evil and must be avoided at all cost. It will rip out your very soul and replace it with a ball of wickedness and evil like you have never seen or felt before."

Mr. Kulicki's eyes flashed over to Lily, Ophelia and Bob.

"Especially you, young'uns. Stay far away from it."

Lily heard thunder again, this time a little closer. Ophelia slipped her arm through Lily's. Katie got up from her seat and lit more lamps to brighten the shadowy parlor, since the dusky evening was darkening.

Suddenly, a lightning bolt exploded right outside the parlor window, lighting up the parlor brighter than a sunny afternoon for a second. Thunder boomed forcefully over the mansion, making the walls shake. Immediately, Lily felt the same dreadful tingling sensation deep in her stomach that she had felt at the cathedral when Miss Josephine appeared.

With surprising speed, Mr. Kulicki jumped to his feet, shook his fist in the air and bellowed, "LEAVE THIS HOUSE, DAUPHINE! Leave and never return, or I shall go to the table of King Clovis himself! Be gone with you!"

He swirled his aged hand in the air as if spinning the air itself. Lily could see that everyone in the room was frightened and was thankful to have Mr. Kulicki handling the situation.

Instantly, the air thickened and whirled, sucking up ash from the unlit fireplace and sprinkling it in heavy doses around each person in the parlor. The floor of the entire room was quickly covered in a coat of black ash.

CRACK! BOOM!

With a brilliantly bright flash, a bolt of lightning shot from the sky down the chimney, instantly engulfing the dry wood in red and yellow flames and shooting sparks out at Lily and her friends.

"Ouch!", Ophelia cried.

"Woah!"

Again, the terribly loud peal of thunder shook the foundation and walls of the house. Somehow the electricity from the storm sucked the room's ashy thick air up and out into the dusky night.

Silence covered the parlor like a thick blanket as they all waited for an explanation from Mr. Kulicki. The sudden transition from the overwhelmingly loud thunder to the complete, dead silence of the room was disorienting. In the silence, Lily noticed that the floor was trembling ever so slightly and the crystal chandelier was softly tinkling.

Mr. Kulicki stayed standing, looking towards the window.

"It's back," he murmured quietly. "The dragon is back."

"What are you talking about, my friend? I don't understand," Otto asked, standing up slowly and walking towards the window. "What dragon?"

"Annabelle's dragon."

"Annabelle's dragon?"

Mr. Kulicki looked at Otto blankly.

"Mrs. Annabelle's dragon," he said with a slight frown, as if Otto had forgotten the name of the family pet. "Draycon, her dragon. Do you not remember, my boy?"

Otto stared blank-faced at Mr. Kulicki for a long moment. No one else spoke. After realizing Mr. Kulicki did not feel the need to elaborate, Otto spoke up again.

"My friend, I have not lost my marbles, and I have never known about any dragon - much less Annabelle's dragon. And now you claim that my own sister evidently became friends with one? Surely you jest."

Mr. Kulicki stared back at Otto for a few seconds.

"I am sorry, my friend. I was quite certain Mrs. Annabelle would have told you."

"Continue," Otto said, frowning deeply.

"Well," Mr. Kulicki replied with a slight smile on his face, "it was right after I came to this home. She was but a small child, but I immediately knew upon meeting the young scamp that I would have to keep a keen eye on her and her mischief.

"Well, one afternoon, I found her in the garden quietly standing before the great tree she called Grandpa Oak, staring up into the branches with a pretty smile on her tiny face. I slipped behind another tree silently and watched her; I did not want to scare away whatever she was so fascinated with.

"But, to my great surprise, it was not a bird nor squirrel as I imagined. T'was a small dragon with bright, red feathers and shiny, white skin – it looked like a newborn, if I could guess, but I was not very educated in the lifecycle of dragons."

Mr. Kulicki cocked his head to one side, deep in thought. "At first, I thought it was some kind of tropical bird or parrot. However, it scrambled from its perch high in the tree to a branch hanging right over Mrs. Annabelle's head, then leaned over and purred like a kitten into her young face, and that was when I realized it was but a dragon. *Then*, with its long tail wrapped around the branch, it started spitting out little puffs of smoke, as if it felt it had to confirm for me that it was, in fact, a dragon.

"Well, she reached out her hands and the little fella jumped right into her arms. It was the strangest thing I ever did see." Mr. Kulicki chuckled. "Sitting down on the ground beneath Grandpa Oak she began humming a tune to the little thing. Before I knew it, she and the dragon had eased back onto the soft earth and fallen asleep. Well, I couldn't leave them there - I knew the little dragon's mother would soon come looking for it. So, I myself stayed right there watching over them for some time. Then, while Mrs. Annabelle was still snoring, the little thing suddenly lifted its head and cocked it to the side, and in a flash took off racing from branch to branch to the top of the oak tree, where it gave itself a push and flew off towards the distant mountains. I walked over to little Mrs. Annabelle and shook her gently. She woke up with a start, looked around, and asked me if I had seen her new kitten.

"'Well, I did see a small white animal; is that what you are talking about?' I asked. She said yes, and I told her it's mother had called it for supper. That seemed to please her, so we returned to the house. But from that day forward, we would both go out to the gardens once a week and visit it; and in no time at all, that thing grew to be quite large. She named it Draycon - Draycon the *Kitten*, she often said - and I went right along with it. Not too many years ago, after Mrs. Annabelle married and her dear Natty passed on, her and I found Draycon dead in the cemetery under the giant oak tree. Sadly, in his large claw, he was still holding the arrow that brought him down to the grave.

"'What do we do, Mr. Kulicki?' Mrs. Annabelle had asked me. I did not know how to answer her.

"Let me think, Mrs. Annabelle,' I said. "We waited for some time in silence as I searched my brain for an answer. However, as we stood trying to think of how to move such a large animal, the day became brighter with sunshine, all the creatures in the graveyard suddenly became silent, and then little by little, that enormous dragon slowly faded into the sunlight.

"Annabelle wept loudly for her pet and swore to find whoever had taken him away from her. That following winter, she came to me early in the morning and told me she had spoken with Draycon's spirit, who apparently had come to her during the night. She said that he had told her where he – the spirit – was staying, and that he was hiding a treasure for her, but his spirit left her before she could gather all the details. The only hint he mentioned was that he had left an ancient map of the Dragon's Lair mountains under Grandpa Oak. We ran to Grandpa Oak that day, but the map wasn't there; much to Mrs. Annabelle's dismay."

Mr. Kulicki paused. Lily looked around the room. Everyone else seemed as baffled as she was. Why hadn't Annabelle said anything to her?

"Huh," Otto said.

Lily couldn't tell if he was shell-shocked or if he didn't believe the story.

"Yes," Mr. Kulicki continued, looking out the window, "so now, because of his love for her, today Draycon is mourning. It was Draycon's purring we heard today, and it was he who caused the thunder and lightning over the distant hills. He has returned to take vengeance on whoever took Mrs. Annabelle's life."

The parlor was still deathly quiet.

"Well," Mr. Kulicki said in a quiet voice, "I must be about my duties."

He stood and walked slowly towards the parlor entrance. As he passed Lily, he mumbled in a quiet whisper, "Guard the crown with your life."

Surprised, Lily turned her head and watched the old gentleman leave the room. He seemed to have aged into an older man since Annabelle had died.

Lily looked at Ophelia, Ophelia looked at Bob and Bob looked at both of them.

"We must find the crown," he whispered softly.

6

Along came a Dragon

GONG. GONG. GONG.

The grandfather clock echoed throughout the house, boldly announcing midnight's arrival.

GONG. GONG. GONG.

Silent flashes of white light burst through the window and illuminated the room around Lily and Ophelia as their minds slipped into the lucid edge of slumber, letting go of their surroundings.

GONG. GONG. GONG.

Thunder clapped in the distance, rippling like waves across the night sky.

GONG. GONG. GONG.

Lily and Ophelia lay snuggled deeply within the fluffy goose-feather comforter of the big four-poster bed, thankful to be in such a comfortable bed instead of traveling in a leaky, damp, lurching stagecoach.

Between flashes of lightning, flickering moon beams slipped past giant tree branches through their bedroom windows, throwing shadowy shades of imaginary creatures dancing on the walls and floorboards. Dark, angry clouds brawled with each other in the night sky before being swept away by a strong west wind, leaving behind a clear, star-filled night.

Pffff.

Small tendrils of gray smoke slipped under the bedroom door, unnoticed by the girls. The odor of sulfur and smoke pulled Ophelia out of her lucid dreams, but not fully – she did not open her eyes, believing the smell to be a remnant of her dreams.

The sound of a creaking door tried to pull Lily out of her sleep but could not. Deep in her dreams, Lily felt that someone was present in their bedroom, but felt unable to escape the scenes playing out in her dream-thoughts.

Tap.

Sharp pricks rapped on Lily's forehead.

Tap. Tap.

A deep, gravelly voice broke the silence.

"Lily Quinn," it said, with a demanding tone.

Tap. Tap. Tap.

These were a little harder than before. She felt her mind pull her out of her dreams against her will. Frustrated, Lily swiped at whatever it was, and buried her head deeper beneath the comforter.

Then she smelled the smoke. She replayed the deep, gravelly voice in her head. *Someone is in the room*, she thought to herself. *It better not be Miss Josephine's ghost*. Without moving, she frantically searched her memory of the room to think of what she could defend herself with. With adrenaline flooding her body, she opened her eyes.

And... there he was, standing over her, looking her square in the eyes – a dragon! She stared at the beast; her eyes as big as saucers.

"Ah, yes," the beast rumbled again. His deep voice reminded Lily of the sound of pebbles and gravel rubbing against each other. "You are the Lily Quinn I am supposed to find! You have the eyes of gold dust, just as she said!"

As Lily wondered if it would be better to have seen Miss Josephine in this room instead of a dragon – after all, she had never met a dragon before - she felt Ophelia's hand grab her arm and squeeze tightly. She could hear her own heart thundering in her chest.

Words failed her as she stared at him, taking everything in. It's skin was scaly and green, with a hint of gold. His enormous wings were tucked in close to his body, except for the one tip of his front paw he had used to tap her on the forehead. The enormous black tip of his claw was still poised, ready to thump her awake again. A double row of horns, which looked like bleached-out bones grew out of his back, reaching from the top of his head to the tip of his tail, where they morphed into one huge barb. Its face was just as scaly as its body. His long, narrow snout came to a snub where his huge nostrils flared, wisps of smoke puffing out every time he spoke. Lily could not see them, but she knew his mouth was full of massive, sharp teeth.

She took this all in quickly, trying to avoid making eye contact, because his eyes were the most frightening. They were fiery-red and huge; their centers seemed to be made of flickering flames. Each as big as Lily's head, or so it seemed, they stared intensely into her very soul.

Stammering and stuttering in a small, squeaky voice, Lily managed to whisper.

"Who are you, and what do you want?"

"I am *Bijou* the dragon," the beast growled indignantly. Immediately he puckered his mouth like a fish and jerked his massive head back, frowning and ruffling his scales upward, obviously insulted. It seemed he thought she should know full well who he was.

"Bijou the *Green Storm!*"

Leaning down again, the huge beast pressed its snout against Lily's nose. She could see right up his flared nostrils as smoke blew onto her face. He paused there for a moment before withdrawing a little to speak again.

"Look closely, my dear. Take a good, long gander at me," Bijou said. The words rumbled from deep within his massive chest, and hot, sulfuric breath filled the air. He squinted, staring directly into her soul.

"Have you not seen me in your dreams," he asked. "In your visions, your nightmares, and your daymares?" He slithered his head along the edge of the bed until his pursed lips were flapping within an inch of Lily's face.

"You do not remember me?"

"No," she said, trembling. Instinctively, Lily reached out and pushed the enormous, scaly head away from her face. "Please," she gasped, "move away a bit."

"Oh, sorry," he said, the scales on his face reddening as if he were embarrassed.

"I just ate a whole field of garlic. I roasted it quickly in my own fire, and it was *quite* tasty," he rumbled. He stuck out his long, slithery tongue and licked his lips. "It was quite potent as well," he said, slurping.

"Well, no, I've never seen you before this very moment," Lily mumbled, covering her mouth with the edge of the blanket. Bijou pulled his head back indignantly and puffed out his goliath chest, once again looking offended.

"Well," he huffed, "I am extremely discombobulated. Everyone who is anyone knows of me!" He paused as if thinking deeply. "You must be a Yankee! Yes! You are a Yankee! I am quite gobsmacked! Well, Yankee-gal, let me show you what I can do."

He stood up as straight as possible. Lily felt Ophelia move the covers down below her eyes so she could see. Bijou seemed a bit cramped for his height, seeing that his head was still bent down almost to his enormous stomach. Opening his huge mouth, he breathed in so forcefully it would have pulled off the bedcovers if Lily and Ophelia had not kept a firm grip on them. Then, he arched his spine back and held his breath; he began to shake like a leaf quivering in a storm. The scales all over his body sprang straight up, and out from beneath each scale burst a puff of bright green smoke. This instantly filled the room with the smell of wet grass, dirt, honeysuckle blossoms, and a slight hint of garlic. The smoke swirled around the room until Bijou, now blue-faced, let out his breath with a mighty *whoosh*. When he did, the green smoke was sucked back into his scaly body. He bent over and looked at the girls again, gasping loudly.

"Well, what do you think about that?" he asked.

"I'm impressed," Lily spluttered quietly. "What do you use that smoke screen for? It smelled rather lovely."

Bijou bent over even closer and glared into Lily's eyes - so close she could count his extremely long nose hairs.

"Lovely? You say it smelled lovely?" he snorted, frustrated. "It smells repulsive!"

"No, not really," Lily whispered timidly.

The dragon stuck its tongue out so far it brushed against Lily's nose, and *poot!* - sprayed spit all over her face. Lily blinked a few times, wiped the spit off her face with the edge of the comforter and sat up in bed with an angry sigh. She puckered her own mouth, stuck out her tongue and *pooted* right back at him.

"Well now," Bijou laughed loudly, "that was mighty pathetic!"

"Okay, Green Bijou," Lily said with as much bravado as she could muster, "stop it this instant. Why are you here in our room, and what do you want from us?"

"Us?" Bijou asked as he looked closely at the bed. "Oh! There's another head in there! Who may this be? Maybe your good friend Opal – er, Otis – ah, Ophelia! That's it, Ophelia Knudson! Hello Ophelia!" The beast leaned right over Lily, got close to Ophelia's face and whispered, "Are you shaking under those blankets because of *me*, my dear? You better be, 'cuz I'm a *dragon!*" he whispered emphatically with a frown on his mug.

"No," Ophelia whispered timidly, "I am not frightened by you."

"Well, you should be!" the dragon almost shouted then snickered with an evil laugh rising up from deep within its chest and... if possible, it looked as if the beasts huge mouth curled into a grin, "I can fry you up like a Sunday chicken dinner with all the fixins' if I've a mind to!"

"Green Bijou!" Lily exclaimed boldly. "What do you want?"

He stared at her with a look of dumb silence; as if she had pulled him out of a spell. His enormous mouth dropped open and his tongue hung off his teeth at one side of his mouth. He was frowning, apparently trying to remember why he was standing in their room.

"Hmmm," he muttered, closing his mouth and smacking his enormous lips while tapping his black claw on his lower lip. "Oh, yeah! I remember." Back to himself, his red eyes met Lily's, and he glared, surprised she would be so bold as to question a dragon.

"For one thing, don't call me *Green Bijou*. Only my enemies call me that. Call me Bijou. But anyway," he paused briefly, continuing to look her in the eyes. "I came to relay a message to you. When you feel the earth tremble violently and you hear the cries of the dragons echo across the sky, run to our mountain."

With that said, he shuffled around a bit and turned towards the door. He started fitting his massive body and backside through the door with difficulty before turning his head and giving them what he thought was a ferocious glare.

"*Bijou,*" Lily called out, "if you're a ghost, why can't you go through the walls or windows instead of pushing yourself through that small door?"

"Who told you I was a ghost?" he snorted as he continued squeezing himself uncomfortably out the door. "I'm a real, live human. Well, make that a real-live dragon! Oh - and by the way - I guess you will have to tell Buford, um, Ben – wait, no, I mean Barney – well, whatever his name is - oh yeah, Bob! Bob! You'll have to tell Bob what I just told you. I am *not* traipsing down these tiny halls looking for him."

GONG.

The clock struck half-past midnight as the dragon continued struggling to push himself out the door.

POP!

Finally, he fell into the hallway and landed in a heap on the floor. He rolled around a bit, grunting and groaning until he managed to get up on his feet. Straightening up as much as he could, Bijou let out a house-shaking fart and sat back down on his haunches, sighing with a look of relief.

Lily looked at Ophelia, and Ophelia looked at Lily. They flopped back on the bed and burst out laughing - until the nasty smell found its way across the room and into their bed, making them lift the covers over their noses.

"*Shut up*," Bijou hissed gravelly from the hallway. They couldn't see him any longer, until suddenly he poked his head back into their room with a despicable scowl on his long face. Smoke shot out his huge nostrils which each panting breath. His eyes furrowed as he frowned.

Flash!

Out from his nostrils shot a long, skinny burst of flames that stopped the girls' laughter and made them dive all the way under the covers. With a thud of his massive tail and a deep grumble in his chest Bijou flew straight out through the closed hallway window without leaving a single crack in its pane. Lily could hear him talking to himself as he left as the two girls jumped up and rushed into the hallway.

"I would fry those Yankee girls, if only I were allowed..." His voice trailed off as he flew away.

"That *was* a ghost!" they exclaimed in unison.

Not a few moments later, thunder rippled across the midnight sky once again, and the rain came down in buckets. Shortly, both girls were asleep again.

7

Through the old Cemetery

Shades of purple and grey appeared in the early morning sky.

Before the hot Mississippi sun had awoken for the day, Lily and Ophelia slid out of bed, quickly dressing themselves and easing the bedroom door open so they could hunt down Bob. Lily took one step into the hallway and gasped. There he was waiting for them, sitting in the hallway outside their bedroom door as if it were the normal thing to do.

"What took you two so long?" he whispered.

"Long?" Lily replied in a whisper, "The sun isn't even up yet!"

"I know, that's the reason we need to get up!"

"Why do you say that?" Lily cocked her head to one side as she looked at him.

"*Well*," Bob answered slowly, "we need to go find out more about this crown all these humans and ghosts are hunting. If it belongs to Otto, Esabella and me it needs to be returned to us!"

"Did you see the dragon last night?" Ophelia blurted out.

"Dragon? Where would I see a dragon? Did y'all see one?"

"Yes," Ophelia stated matter-of-factly. "And he said to tell you everything he told us!"

"Well, what did it say?"

"It told us to run for the dragons' mountain when we feel the earth tremble and hear the cries of the dragons echoing across the farmland."

For a moment, Bob was expressionless, which surprised both the girls. Then, frowning, Bob spoke firmly.

"Okay, but don't tell anyone about this. Don't tell Otto, Esabella, Katie, or even Mr. Kulicki, okay?"

Taken aback by his stern look, Lily and Ophelia merely nodded their heads in agreement.

"I smell bacon," Ophelia whispered. "I'm hungry."

They slipped down the stairs and into the kitchen and, to their surprise, found Otto and Katie. Katie was serving Otto eggs and bacon on the small kitchen table, and Otto was pouring over his paperwork. Mr. Kulicki came in from the back porch just as the three of them entered from the hall.

"Good morning!" Otto boomed in his usual, jovial voice. "What are you gals up to so early this lovely morning?"

They didn't answer. Lily and Ophelia quickly sat down at the table and reached for the eggs and bacon as Bob stood by the dry sink with a plate in his hands.

"Hold on there," Otto boomed, glaring at Lily and Ophelia with a twinkle in his eye. "I asked you a question. Now, don't you gals be getting into any foolishness today. Miss Kate and I are planning our nuptials but first we must plan a celebration of Annabelle's life. What do you say about that?"

"Nuptials?" Lily smiled at Miss Katie and Otto. "I had no idea! That's wonderful!"

"Thank you, Miss Lily," Kate answered softly with a smile.

The back door slammed open loudly, and in walked Mr. Pat and Mr. Porter from the stables. "What a relief," Lily thought. She had no idea what to say to Otto about her plans for this morning. The two men quickly walked to the wash basin, washed their hands and took a seat at the table where they immediately began filling their plates.

"Well, Otto, my boy," Mr. Pat said with a grin, "I'm mighty glad to welcome you into our family! I mean, you have always been our family, but this is a double blessing."

Mr. Pat turned and looked at the girls. "Please pass the bacon, Lily. My stomach is chewing on my backbone!"

She passed him a plate with one hand, using her other hand to scoop more food onto her plate, hardly looking at him as she inhaled her food.

"Thanks, gal!"

"Yoush welco", she said, her mouth so full of food she could hardly speak.

She was suddenly aware that the whole room was silent. She looked up from her plate to see the adults with forks held in midair, all staring at her and Ophelia.

"Slow down there, gals," Mr. Pat said, almost laughing. "Ain't nobody gonna take that food from ya. You might just choke on it!"

"Sorry," Lily whispered awkwardly. She felt her face turn bright red. Ophelia, who had not stopped eating, snickered. She slowed down, but only a little. In no time at all, they both had lapped up the last bit of their food. Excusing themselves, they walked over to Bob by the dry sink then washed their plates, then their hands, then darted out the door onto the back porch. There they filled their pockets with apples from an apple barrel before flying down the back steps in a quick escape from prying adults.

"Whew, that was a close one," Lily said, relieved. "I didn't know what to say to Otto without lying."

"Me too," Ophelia replied. "I was eating as fast as I could, but Lily, your face was almost resting on the side of your plate!"

"Yeah," Lily laughed. "When Mr. Pat said that, I realized I probably looked like a pig at the slop trough."

"Come on," Bob whispered, "let's go into the cemetery and check it out. See if we can find anything, or anybody else."

The three of them stopped alongside the rusty wrought-iron fence of the cemetery. Ophelia turned and looked at Bob closely.

"Bob, I'm curious, why is it that Otto never says a word to you? Why didn't he ask *you* what you were doing today?"

Bob stood looking through the fence in silence for a minute before looking down at his feet.

"I don't really know," he replied in a seemingly sad whisper.

Neither Lily nor Ophelia could think of anything to say. The three stood in silence for a while before Lily broke it with a whisper.

"Well, shall we go through the cemetery, Bob?"

"Sure," he whispered back, nodding his head.

"Why are we whispering?" Ophelia asked.

"Because," Bob said quietly, "the dead can hear us, you know."

"No, they can't," Ophelia said.

"Oh, yes they can. How do you think they know when a living human enters a cemetery? They hear humans and come out to see what they are up to. During a funeral they don't usually bother because they already know what's going on."

"How do you know that?" Lily asked.

"I just do. It's common sense, isn't it?"

"Not to me," Ophelia said. "I think it's creepy that you know so much about the skeletons and such. Who tells you all this?"

Bob looked at Ophelia as if she was from outer space.

"It just makes sense, doesn't it?" he asked again.

Ophelia snorted, looking intensely at Bob. "Are you a ghost?"

"What? Look at me! Do I look like a ghost? Do I feel like a ghost?"

Ophelia snorted again. Lily was quiet.

"Come on," Lily whispered. "Let's go. We can go through the cemetery. Do you mind, Ophelia?"

"Nope," Ophelia replied. "As long as we have *Bob the Ghost* with us, I don't think anything will bother us."

"Humph!" Bob snorted.

"Where *are* we going, Bob?"

"Through the cemetery to the Dragon mountains. It's the easiest way to get there"

Lily and Ophelia stopped in their tracks and looked at Bob.

"The dragon said to come when we felt the earth tremble and heard the dragon's cry."

"Come on," Bob turned and looked at them. "Let's go and check it out. I promise we won't go into the mountain itself."

Hesitating for only a few seconds, Lily and Ophelia agreed with Bob.

After squeezing through the rusty cemetery gate again and running all the way to the far end of the large cemetery, the three walked single file along the nearly invisible path that took them closer and closer to Dragons' Mountain. The lack of trees on the upward climb allowed the now sweltering sun to beat mercilessly down upon their heads. They struggled up the narrow, weed-covered path with sweaty faces and labored breathing. It seemed to grow steeper and steeper as they continued. Eventually it seemed the path had turned almost vertical with the side of the mountain. The three were definitely struggling.

Stretching and scrambling for some type of a handhold Bob, being the first in line, grabbed ahold of a large root sticking out of the ground. He pulled himself up over the edge of the path and onto a flat plateau, then turned and helped Lily and Ophelia make their way up as well. All three lay on their backs gasping for air. They were lying on a large, tree-covered plateau half way up the mountain. The plateau must have encompassed an area of ten acres or more, or so it seemed. Looking upwards at the top of the mountain behind the plateau, they could see snow covered peaks and every few seconds large puffs of smoke blew from its white, icy summit. The gusting winds at its top were visible as it blew and swirled snow around its peaks and valleys. They could see no path leading to its summit but they could see where the tree line ended due to diminishing oxygen.

"I don't think we should try and reach the top!" Lily stated, "In fact, Bob, if you want to go right ahead because I'm not going up there. Are you Ophelia?"

"Heck no"

"Neither am I", Bob stated matter-of-factly, "I've been...er...tried that before and I'm not doing it again."

"Look, you can see almost all of the Mississippi delta from here," Ophelia said, rolling onto her stomach.

The three looked out in amazement. Not only could they see the entire village of Vicksburg, they could see well beyond the Mississippi river and into Arkansas. It had taken much longer than Bob had anticipated for them to get to Dragons' Mountain, but to Lily, the view was well worth the exhausting climb.

They pulled themselves to their feet and turned to face the mountain. It seemed enormous beyond belief. Lily had seen this mountain on the horizon many times while running the streets of Vicksburg, but had never realized how magnificent it was. Up close now, it seemed to Lily the mountain was almost alive, that some mystery surrounded it. It was unsettling.

Even more unsettling was the complete lack of sound within the plateau. Not one bird, frog or cricket could be heard, even though giant Banyan trees, thick and twisted together like an enormous puzzle, filled the plateau. Spanish moss hung so thickly from each branch that there was barely enough room for an animal to slip through. Some were long enough to brush the ground or wrap around the trunk of a tree.

Stepping behind Bob, Lily gave him a nudge.

"What now?"

"Well," Bob whispered confidently, "let's go through the plateau and see what's on the other side."

Seeing no worn paths leading through the forest, their only choice was to push through the hanging moss. The floor of the forest was clear of small brush and weeds, so all they had to deal with was the thick, hanging moss.

As they made their way forward, a soft, almost inaudible wind swept through the trees, moving the moss away from their path and making it possible to see a large gap within the dense forest.

Lily and Ophelia stood stone-still.

"This ain't right, Lily," Ophelia mumbled quietly.

Lily shushed her. "Something knows we're here," Lily whispered.

Bob had not stopped when the moss parted the forest greenery. Instead, he picked up his pace. Did he know something Lily did not? He was now about twenty steps into the forest in front of them, walking quickly through the open, moss-lined tunnel.

"Bob!" Lily whispered loudly, "Hey! Wait up!"

He didn't even look back at them. In fact, he began jogging.

"Bob!" Ophelia called out.

Grabbing Ophelia's hand, Lily stopped her friend from calling out again.

"Shh, something isn't right here," Lily whispered in a slightly frightened voice.

"Ya think?" Ophelia replied sarcastically, bugging out her eyes.

In what seemed to be slow motion, the Spanish moss began creeping back into place right behind Bob's fleeing figure, even as he was full-on sprinting through the forest. Soon the two girls were surrounded by gently swaying moss skimming across their faces, as if it were alive and trying to recognize them by touch.

It was an eerie feeling. Shivers ran up and down Lily arms as she aggressively pushed the moist, dewy tendrils away from her body. She peered back towards the path leading down into the delta; it was now covered with shadow.

Reluctant to walk any further into the forest, Ophelia also looked back at the path, then forward to the mountain, then back to the path, then again to the mountain. She kept doing this until Lily shook her head, obviously annoyed, and walked ahead into the moss-covered trees.

Not wanting to be left behind with night coming on, Ophelia scurried to catch up with Lily, mumbling in protest as she made her way through the hanging moss.

"I don't know why I keep following you on these crazy, dangerous adventures. I'm gonna have to get a different friend who is more *normal*. One of these times we aren't going to get away from these haints and skeletons, and then they'll pull us down into wherever they stay and our folks will find our mangled bodies all decayed and rotting in some swamp with the alligators and snakes and worms crawling in and out of our eyeball sockets!"

"I'm normal," Lily replied.

"Hah! You're about as normal as a hyena at the Queen's tea party."

Lily ignored Ophelia and kept walking further into the woods. They continued for what

seemed to be an eternity, pulling sticky, clinging moss off their faces. After a long time, Lily could suddenly see the side of the enormous mountain in front of them, maybe fifty feet ahead. The sound of murmuring voices and a crackling fire reached her ears. She could smell smoke.

Motioning for Ophelia to stay quiet, the two of them crept closer to the voices. Skulking halfway there, they eased behind a large tree and peeked around its trunk. There, sitting around a blazing firepit were thirty or so skeletons, ghosts, and flesh-and-blood humans. Lily scanned the group from left to right.

"Where's Bob?"

"Look, Lily! There's Fartin' Freddie's ghost, and there's - what's his name? The ghost who showed up at Katie Pirogue's house. You know, the one Granny Pirogue told Katie to summon?

"Tree-Top Teddy?" Lily scanned the group around the firepit.

"Yep, that's him, right there beside Fartin' Freddie!" Ophelia giggled quietly. "And there's the magpie peeping out of Teddy's stove-pipe hat."

"Ophelia, look! It's Peg-Leg Paddy McGee – the one we saw with Ott and Paul!"

As the girls scanned the group from left to right, they realized something.

"Bob isn't here!" they said in unison.

"Where is he?" Ophelia asked.

"I'm not sure," Lily replied. She stared at Peg-Leg, trying to think of where Bob could have gone. As Lily stared at Peg-Leg, he turned his head and seemed to be starting right back at them.

"I think those creatures can see us," Lily whispered. "Peg-Leg seems to be looking right at us."

"I sure hope not," Ophelia whispered back. "Maybe these trees are see-through. This place is a weird place to be. What do ya think?"

Lily slipped her head behind the trunk of the tree and picked at the bark. It came off in chunks so she was quite sure it was a real tree.

"I'm thinking maybe they feel our presence. I don't think they can see us. At least I hope they can't."

The large fire was blazing in a shallow pit close to the mountain's granite wall, and the ghosts were seated on that side of the circle. The granite was made of vertical streaks of black and grey rock; green vines and other creeping plants poked their fingers through the small holes and dents in the wall, apparently trying to reach the ground. Small embers caught the tips of the vines, but sputtered out since the plants were damp.

The ghosts didn't seem to mind the flames; in fact, they appeared to enjoy the heat. Some were lounging leisurely around the fire with their feet and legs resting in the hot embers as they leaned back against the solid wall. One ghost, who Lily did not recognize, was all stretched out with one hand behind his head and the other hand holding a cigar in its ghostly mouth, puffing out smoke rings, one right after the other. On the right side of the cigar smoker sat the ghost of the enormous grizzly bear called *Banshee*. It was sitting on its haunches slowly moving its head from side to side as if anxiously waiting for something to happen. On the left side of the cigar smoker sat none other than one of those red-haired haints from up north in the state of Michigan Lily and Ophelia had ran into in one of their previous adventures.

Lily wasn't sure if the red-haired haint was a man or woman, but she guessed it was a woman. Her wild red hair was floating around her head in a lazy manner as if she was asleep. Every red-haired haint Lily had ever seen before had hair that twisted and swirled around its head like it was being blown by a strong wind. This haint had an extremely long tongue - which every red-haired haint was known to have - hanging out and every so often would slap its tongue at a bug clinging to the creeping vines, grab hold of it and fling it into the flames with a quick flick of its tongue, where it vanished with a loud *POP.*

On the left side of the firepit sat the skeletons. There was Nevil Bindi, who had stolen Chauncey Jenkins' bag of gold dust back in Sydney, Australia, and his friend Archie Bald Crumb who was still sucking his thumb bone. Next to Archie Bald sat his wife Anthelia, holding a bottle of rum in each hand. Next to Anthelia sat a couple of skeletons Lily and Ophelia had never seen before, as well as the skeleton of an old seadog named Scallywags Scruggs who had been seen riding the waves of the ocean like he was riding a horse. He was a scruffy old skeleton, and if Lily remembered correctly, Phineas Pennypacker had told her Scallywags was a ghost, not a skeleton. Maybe, Lily thought, he was demoted from being a ghost down to being a skeleton for some reason. Skeletons were at the bottom of the barrel, so to speak, of the dead realm.

Lastly, on the right side of the firepit sat flesh-and-bone humans. To Lily and Ophelia's shock, sitting amongst the humans was none other than Miss Josephine herself, dressed entirely in black, with a thin, see-through veil over her face. Miss Josephine stared intently at the spot where the girls were hiding, but quickly darted her eyes away and turned her head towards the mountain wall. The blood in Lily and Ophelia's veins ran cold as ice.

Next to Miss Josephine sat three woman who looked to be gypsies, and next to them sat a man Lily recognized as Ragman Rufus. Ragman Rufus traveled a yearly circuit from St. Louis to Vicksburg, Mississippi and back, gathering rags, bones and metal scrap to sell along the way to anyone willing to buy. Ragman Rufus and the old gypsy woman seemed to be well acquainted; they had their heads bent down, talking quickly to each other in hushed voices.

Suddenly, two men walked out of the forest, joining the group. They plopped themselves down between Fartin' Freddie and another ghost.

"Chauncey Jenkins and Shadrack Jones," Lily exclaimed softly.

"Go over *there* with the other flesh and bone scabs," Freddie shouted at them. "Don't come over here unless you're dead!"

"Yeah!" A volley of yells from the rest of the ghosts and skeletons joined him. Even Banshee bellowed.

Shadrack and Chauncey instantly jumped up and hustled over to sit down beside Miss Josephine, who immediately gave Chauncey a hard shove. "Move your filthy body away from me! Go sit by the filthy, stinkin' gypsy pig in the red dress!'

Calmly but firmly, the old gypsy woman spoke up, her head still hanging down as if it were difficult for her to lift it. "I be no stinkin', bawlow, gypsy, ya devil woman. I shall cast a Romany curse on you and put your sorry, dinlow soul into a frog and then I am gonna punt you into the yog!"

"Shut-up, old woman," Miss Josephine said loudly with a snarly sneer on her face, "I will send your filthy bones flying so high into the night sky you will never be seen again!"

The old gypsy; crippled by twisted and disfigured bones, stared into the flames for a minute or two. Then, with great effort, she struggled to her feet, staggered a bit, then put her hands on her bony hips. Turning to face Miss Josephine, slowly and calmly she reached into her shirt pocket and took out a pouch, which immediately began to shimmer and glow bright red. With great care she pulled the drawstrings open, tipped the glowing pouch a bit and poured some kind of substance into her gnarly, wrinkled hand. Lily couldn't see what it was. The old gypsy mumbled a few Romany sentences, now tightly grasping the powder from the pouch; red smoke seeped between her tightly squeezed fingers and floated into the air. Then, with the speed of lightning, she opened her hand, and as quick as a flash, she flung the sparkling red powder across Miss Josephine 's face, and into the

130

fire. Instantly Miss Josephine let out a screech and turned into a transparent, human-sized frog, and was swopped into the flames. Slowly she melted into the embers, which were now burning bright blue. After a moment, the small blue flame burst into the night sky with a loud *snap*, and vanished.

The gathering around the firepit became as silent as a tomb. The gypsy stumbled a bit as she sat back down and stared into the flames. Everyone stared at her, afraid for their lives. Calmly the old woman lifted her wrinkled face and revealed snaggled teeth as she smiled.

"Aye," she said slowly in a soft whisper as she nodded her head. "'Tis not so bad a thing to be gone of a devil, now is it, lads?" Not one soul replied to her. Everyone stood staring open-mouthed, their faces full of fear.

"Aye!" Shadrack exclaimed, awkwardly breaking the silence. "Aye, 'tis a good thing, I say! Right lads?"

The rest of the group looked at each other for a second or two. Suddenly it was as if Lily could see the lights coming on in their brains as they all began cheerfully agreeing with the old gypsy.

"Aye!"

"Aye, ma'am! 'Tis a great thing!"

"One less of us to get the crown, I say!" yelled out Nevil Bindi.

"Aye!" The rest answered his statement in unison.

Chauncey and Shadrack plopped down right where they were, stretched out their legs, leaned back and sighed deeply. Chauncey leaned close to Shadrack's ear and whispered, "I'm powerful glad that old gypsy woman is here."

"Hey!" Nevil Bindi yelled abruptly across the flames at Chauncey. "I want that bag of gold you took from me. I stole it fair and square over in Sydney!"

"It's mine, ya stupid bag of bones!" Chauncey called back. "You stole it off'en my neck!"

"But I stole it fair and square!"

"Ya pushed me into the street in front of a twelve-mule team then jerked it off'en my neck as I went down! That's not *fair and square*, mate! Besides, there ain't no such thing as stealing fair and square! Stealing is stealing, and if ya get caught, ya gotta pay the piper and give it back!"

Nevil stood up and leaned across the flames. Chauncey did too.

"I'll fight ya for it," Nevil yelled, grinning.

"Whatcha gonna do with it, baggy-bones? You're a skel-tin. Ya can't spend it, 'cuz ain't nobody would take gold off'en a skel-tin!"

"When I find that crown and get my body back, I can spend it most anywhere I want. So, I want it back!" Nevil then took one step into the flames, then another, and another; suddenly, he was standing face to face with Chauncey.

Chauncey did not hesitate. He gave Nevil a hard shove, and down he went into the firepit where he rolled around a bit before scrambling to his feet. His leg and arm bones were black with soot; tiny, flickering sparks snapped and popped on the back of his skull.

By this time every creature around the fire was standing up, loudly cheering one of them on.

"Hit 'em again!" Shadrack yelled out to his friend, his hands cupped around his mouth to make his voice carry further.

"Hit 'em hard upside the noggin, Nevil!" Archie Bald hollered.

"Drag 'em inta the far'!" shouted one of the ghosts. "He's flesh and bone, he cain't survive the far'!"

So many voices were shouting out that Lily couldn't discern who was saying what.

"Whoop 'em good, Nevil!"

"Get 'em, Chauncy!"

A few voices had started chanting.

"Ne-vil! Ne-vil! Ne-vil!"

"Chaun-cey! Chaun-cey!"

"Get 'em, Chauncey, get 'em good! Hit 'em on the neck!" the old gypsy woman shrieked.

Nevil and Chauncey were standing nose to nose, circling each other. Chauncey had his fists raised to his chin, jabbing at Nevil without really touching him; Nevil was dancing a jig in front of Chauncey, ducking and dodging. His arms were flopping everywhere, and his head was bobbing like a fishing line bobbing in the water.

All the creatures were jumping up and down, yelling out loud curses and encouraging their favored competitor. They were now on one side of the firepit with Chauncey and Nevil alone on the other. The gypsy in the red dress seemed to be shouting out curses on Nevil so Chauncey would win. Banshee the grizzly was standing up on his ghostly hind legs roaring loudly with his massive head thrown back so far Lily was sure he was going to fall over backwards, and on his shoulders sat the ghost of the little French boy, Baptiste, urging him on. Baptiste would lean his head back, give a loud yell then Banshee would do the same.

Shadrack Jones, standing back a bit but encouraging Chauncey, was even punching his own fists out in front of himself as if he too were fighting. "Give a left jab, Chauncey! Give him an upper-cut to that bone head!"

The crowd around the fire seemed to be getting more and more rowdy, even though Nevil and Chauncey were not making much progress in their fight.

"Drag 'em in da far'! Drag em' in da far!'" yelled a squeaky voiced ghost that had an arrow sticking through his ghostly ribs. He was jumping up and down with excitement.

"Bust 'em in da chops, mate! I know'd 'em when he was a lil' bugger, an he ain't nothin' but trouble!" shouted a skeleton, obviously from Australia.

"Drag 'em in da far'!"

"Give 'em an upper-cut!"

"Drag 'em in da far'! Drag 'em in da far'! DRAG 'EM IN DA FAR'!" A group of skeletons were chanting and jumping, getting louder with each passing moment. Then, to Lily's surprise, all the ghosts attacked the skeletons at once, and an all-out fracas began. Bones were flying everywhere and somehow the ghosts were losing parts of their snowy white bodies. But, just as quick as it had started, it stopped. The two factions turned back to Chauncey and Nevil, and once again started yelling out encouragements all as one.

"I think this is the ghost rendezvous," Lily said, chuckling.

"But where is Bob?" Ophelia asked, looking around.

"I have no idea," Lily muttered. Lily was much too interested in what was happening directly in front of them to be worrying about Bob.

BOOM!

A huge ball of flames and embers exploded from the center of the firepit. Everyone, including Chauncey and Nevil, stopped and stared at the firepit. When the smoke and ash cleared, there stood the ghost of the old Arch Bishop.

"Look, Lily! Remember the Arch Bishop?" Ophelia asked.

"Wow! Yeah," Lily whispered.

The poor old ghost looked more bedraggled than ever. His fine mitre hat was askew and his fancy robe was tattered and torn. His feet were bare except for one knee-stocking which had fallen around his ankle. Gone were his elaborate staff and jeweled neck ropes.

"QUIET!" The Arch Bishop wheezed, trying his best to bellow. It came out as a wheezy, squeaky yell. It worked though – instantly, the entire group around the firepit quieted. He raised his hand and started to speak.

"I have come, once again, to claim the golden crown which belongs to the royal family. All of you will silently leave and go back to wherever you have come from - be it earth or otherwise."

"Blah, blah, blah," Scallywags Scruggs said loudly. He reached out a long, bony finger, pointed at the Arch Bishop, and yelled. "Leave, old man, so we can finish our quest for the crown!" The entire group began yelling and throwing embers and pieces of wood at the old Bishop. The poor old Bishop sat down in the firepit and hung his head.

Out of the corner of their eyes Lily and Ophelia caught a movement about ten feet from where they were hiding.

Poof!

The girls heard a gentle sound just behind them. A thin puff of smoke slithered unnoticed through the underbrush and dissipated into the night.

Easing down to squat around the bottom of the tree trunk the two of them peered through the thick, lower branches. Staring at the brush with wide eyes, they watched as Bijou's big head emerged from the forest. His eyes were glowing bright-red.

"It's Bijou," Ophelia whispered so softly Lily that could barely hear her.

"Hmmm?" the dragon muttered, quickly whipping his head in their direction. Quietly the two of them jerked away from the tiny opening they had been peering through, hoping Bijou could not see them. They knew if he had seen them, his big mouth would let everyone else know where they were hiding.

Another small tuft of smoke left his nostrils as he turned his massive head back towards the group gathered at the firepit. Slowly, and on his belly, he slithered out from the forest. His snout stayed to the ground as he went, sniffing like a dog finding food, straight to the fire pit. His tail was sticking up in the air like a dog on a trail. Those around him must not have been surprised to see him because not one of them acknowledged that a huge dragon was pushing them out of his way to approach the firepit.

"ENOUGH!" His deep, gravelly voice roared loudly, echoing through the forest as he stood to his full height then bent his head down towards all the creatures. He leaned across the firepit with his head no further than a foot or two from their faces staring in turn at each and every one of them. Everyone instantly became as quiet as church mice.

"I smell burnt frog," he growled deep in his chest. He slithered a little closer to the firepit. Then, shifting his body to the left, he glared at the old gypsy woman with a deep frown.

"Did *you* do it, Delphinia? Did you fry another soul?"

The old gypsy shuffled over to Bijou and stood before him boldly - as straight as her crippled body would allow. "Yes, I did!"

she declared proudly with her hands on her hips. "I did away with that devil-woman." She hesitated before continuing. "What are you going to do about it?"

"No-no-nothing," Bijou stammered, immediately stumbling backwards a bit. "Nothing at all, Delphinia. Nothing at all." He looked down to the ground. Lily was shocked to see such a large dragon so timid before the old woman.

Then, the air changed. The forest became very quiet very quickly. Bijou drew in a sharp breath, looked up towards the night sky and suddenly faded into nothing. The air around the firepit became as cold as ice. Shivering and shaking, Lily could smell sulfur. A strong rustling sound in the branches over her head sent a chill down Lily's spine. They did not want to look, but they could not stop themselves. Lily and Ophelia jerked their heads skyward.

It was horrifying. There above them, hovering in clear view, was the biggest dragon Lily could have ever imagined. The entire beast was ice blue with transparent wings. This contrasted sharply with its eyes, bright and as red as flames. Spikes protruded everywhere along its entire back, from the top of its head to the tip of its tail. Huge red feathers rose high above its head as well as beneath its wings. Its long, enormous tail whipped around in the air behind it; the end of the tail was a mammoth barb, snapping up and down angrily. The dragon's huge wings looked like those of a bat, with tight, leathery skin underneath its bright-red feathers. The wings overshadowed the whole firepit and beyond.

Lily felt her chest tightening with fear. A cold sweat broke out on Ophelia's neck. They could not stop looking at it. The dragon beat its wings in the air, and Lily noticed a sparkle of golden light coming from its neck. She hadn't seen it at first, but now she could clearly - from its neck hung a thick, brilliant, golden chain. It swung back and forth as the dragon flapped its wings. On the end of the chain dangled the coveted golden crown. Lily couldn't believe it.

"How is this real?" She asked herself under her breath.

Lily could feel the tension amongst the thieves and scoundrels around the firepit. She looked over at them for a second. Most of them were staring at the crown. They were not staring at the dragon. They were captivated by the swaying crown. A strong sense of anticipation was thick in the air.

The crown dangled from the dragon's neck like a carrot in front of a horse. The firepit crowd stood frozen in their tracks. Lily wasn't sure if they were stunned from fear, or if they were all individually plotting a way to get the crown and escape.

Lily could hear the dragon taking a deep breath.

"Get down, Ophelia!"

BOOM!

The girls hit the floor and covered their heads with their arms just as the dragon lit up the night with a torrent of flames. The giant beast rained fire down into the firepit, where it exploded with blasts in an enormous ball of flames. Embers, sparks, ash and rocks flew high above all their heads.

Lily's ears were ringing, and her eyes seemed momentarily blinded by the light of the explosion. She regained her vision in a couple seconds, and looked up at the firepit. Jerked from their frozen stupor, every creature had turned and charged for the path leading down the side of the mountain. The ghosts immediately vanished into the night sky, leaving the skeletons and humans behind. They looked like a herd of stampeding buffalo, shouting and jumping over each other as they fled, terrified. Lily heard the dragon start to take a deep breath again.

She did not hesitate for a second. Instinct took over. She jumped to her feet and pulled Ophelia up with her. Ophelia yelled, being pulled right off her feet. "Woah, Lily!"

Dashing down the path in front of the crashing stampede of thieves and scoundrels, the girls raced towards the edge of the plateau, leaving eddies of dust and dirt swirling and spinning behind them in thick, brown clouds. A few of the faster creatures caught up to them quickly and swept past them in a manic rush pushing them into the trees.

"Umph!" The girls groaned as they hit the ground. They had been shoved brutally into the forest by a big-boned skeleton. Lily tried to catch her breath; the fall had knocked the wind out of her.

"Come on, Lily!" Ophelia tried to help her up. As Lily was getting to her feet, the forest all turned a hint of orange.

BOOM!

A second explosion rocked the firepit behind them. It sounded like lightning had struck just behind them. The thunderous noise made Lily's ears ring again. Looking up, she stared for a brief moment at the fleeing thieves. There, passing in front of them, was Chauncey Jenkins with his long legs stretched out in front of him churning up dirt all around him. Shadrack was right behind him, charging like a small elephant.

The echo of the explosion continued to roll through the forest as the orange glow died out. Over the treetops, Lily could see an orange-red fireball from the second explosion back at the firepit.

The rushing crowd was stirring up so much dirt and dust it was becoming difficult for the girls to see an opening in the line in which they could jump back into the mad dash to safety. Suddenly Bijou appeared above the dust clouds, seemingly looking for something in the forest. Just before he passed them, Bijou sidestepped, reached out his front paws and in one sweeping motion grabbed both Lily and Ophelia, flinging them on his back.

"WOAH!" Ophelia shouted.

They each grabbed one of the horns sticking out of his hide, and held on for dear life as he flew up and out of the forest-covered plateau, into the starry night sky. He continued to climb for a minute or so, and then leveled out. The girls could feel their hearts pounding in their throats. Bijou soared for a while without saying a word to either of them. The girls were too fascinated and bewildered at everything that was happening to speak, so they just held tight onto Bijou's horns and gazed down to the earth far below. A sense of calm slowly came back to them. Lily was curious if she could see Shadrack or Chauncey from here, but the fleeing stampede had created a cloud of dust too thick for her to see through.

Bijou seemed to pick up speed. The wind tugged at their hair, causing their braids to loosen and whip around their heads. Suddenly, Bijou began banking hard in different directions, twisting and turning in the darkness. Afraid, the girls held on as tightly as they could as the stars spun around them.

"What are you doing?!?" Lily tried to ask over the roaring wind in her face. Bijou didn't respond. She wasn't sure if he was ignoring her or if he couldn't hear her. She tried again, but he didn't respond.

"WOAH!"

Both the girls gasped as he took a sharp left turn, and their bodies flung to the side, almost falling off him. Right as they regained their balance, he flapped his wings and angled up toward the stars, apparently trying to gain altitude quickly. The air was getting cold.

"STOP IT, BIJOU!" They screamed in unison. He didn't respond.

Lily turned around to look at Ophelia, and then suddenly realized why Bijou was flying so erratically. The huge, icy-blue dragon was chasing them, only a few hundred yards behind.

"What?" Ophelia screamed over the icy wind. "What are you looking at?"

Lily did not have to answer. The blue dragon reared its head back and bellowed a deep, terrifying roar. Immediately, flames filled the air behind them. Ophelia knew what it was without even turning around, because the flames had put an orange hue all over Lily's face and body. The dragon's voice echoed across the immense, black sky, reminding Lily of a lion roaring in the African darkness. It seemed to be closing in on them. Lily could hear her heartbeat in her head. She held onto Bijou's ivory horns as tight as she possibly could; her forearms were burning.

Suddenly, Bijou's body became invisible. It looked as if *they* were now the ones flying – they could see clouds directly beneath them! Only his horns were visible, and only slightly. Was he able to keep his horns visible for their sake? Lily could still feel Bijou's body beneath them, so she knew they were still safely seated – for now. The entire experience was thrilling. Then, just as suddenly, the horns also became invisible and Lily felt a soft covering fold over her and Ophelia. It felt like Bijou was covering them with his wings.

Silently, Bijou floated down towards the Vicksburg mansion where he slowly landed in a grove of trees inside the mansion's cemetery. Bijou instantly became visible again. He unfolded his enormous wings that had been wrapped around them, and sighed deeply.

"Go," he whispered, lowering his neck so the two of them could easily slid off onto the ground. "Don't stop until you are safe." With that, he immediately vanished into the night.

Making sure their shoes would not make noise on the cobblestones the two girls ran quietly but quickly in the grass alongside the pathway, running towards the wrought-iron gate. Every lamppost had flickered out, leaving the moon as the only beacon to guide them to safety. Frosty-white moonbeams cast strange shadows around the looming headstones. The eerie feeling of being watched crept into their souls as they ran, making them run quicker.

"Hey!" came a quick, sharp whisper from behind them.

Jumping with heart-stopping fright, the two girls whirled around. There was Bob, running to meet them.

"What happened to you, Bob?" Lily whispered. "You took off running and we lost sight of you! Did you go to the firepit where all the creepy souls were gathered?"

"Yes," Bob whispered breathlessly, catching his breath.

"Then where in the heck were you? We looked all around that firepit and we sure didn't see you!"

"I saw you; I was hidden in the vines. I know a different way up to the top of the ledge so that's where I went. I went to the ledge, slid down a clump of vines, and that's where I stayed throughout the entire brawl." He chuckled.

"I don't believe you," Ophelia hissed, staring sternly into his eyes. "I think you were out looking for something. And, by the way, how did you get here so quick? We hitched a ride with Bijou. How did you do it?"

"Easy," Bob replied, as he shifted his eyes away from Ophelia. "I hitched a ride with that Scallywags Scruggs fella. I'd met him a time or two before, so he grabbed holt' of me when he flew past, and away we flew. You know, he's not such a bad fella, really."

"Humpf," Lily muttered. The girls stood with arms crossed, staring at Bob for a moment. Then they turned and continued on quickly toward the big gate.

"Come on then, Bob. Bijou told us to hurry up and go home."

In silence the three of them hurried along the path until they were within sight of the gate. Suddenly Lily skidded to a stop and held out her arms to stop the other two.

"Look," she whispered softly. She pointed towards one of the greenhouses built next to the mansion. Tip-toeing behind an enormous headstone she pulled the other two along with her where all three craned their heads around the enormous statue to have a look.

There, beyond the gate, standing next to one of the two large, glass-enclosed greenhouses was a crouched-over shadowy figure cloaked in a long, black, hooded cape. Out from the edges of the hood sprang glowing strands of white hair. The figure had its hands cupped against the window and was peering intently through the glass.

The three of them stood frozen beside the headstone as they watched the peculiar creature shuffle from window to window. Suddenly the creature came to an abrupt stop, straightened slightly, and peered into the darkness toward the cemetery. The face of the creature was hidden beneath the hood but the wild hair was sticking out from around the hood like a fur collar. Not even its eyes could be made out in the darkness, but they could feel it's eyes roaming across the cemetery. It almost seemed as if some kind of lightning or energy was coming out of its eyes. Lily's heart almost stopped beating as she stood peeking at the creature.

Suddenly the creature flung something in their direction.

Pop! Snap!

The headstone they were hiding behind was hit with whatever the creature was flinging out. Smoke filled the air around them, making Lily want to cough. The three of them dove onto the ground.

"What is that?" Bob whispered. "I have never seen one of those creatures before. It must be from a place beyond the realm I'm familiar with."

"I'd say it's way beyond my knowledge," Lily whispered. Ophelia nodded her head in agreement.

"It must be looking for the crown too," Bob muttered quietly.

Silently they scooted their bodies closer to a huge statue and eased their heads around the corner of the headstone's base. The creature was scurrying towards the cemetery gate. It easily slipped between the spindles. Then it bent down and used its long arms as feet, racing past them. As it passed, it turned its head to try to find them. Its hood had fallen back, exposing a mass of silver, glowing hair. It had the head of a long-nosed wolf. Its mouth was hanging open, panting like a dog; its drooling tongue hung out between long, grotesque, jagged teeth. As the beast ran, its drool was so thick it was flying back into the creature's face; leaving globs of bright, glowing saliva hanging off the edges of its facial hair.

"It's a wolftaur," Bob whispered quietly. "It's after the crown, just as I thought."

"How do you know that?" Ophelia whispered back.

"A wolftaur is a dead human who was so evil and vile when they were alive that the jaws of hades grabbed them off the face of the earth and flung them into the body of a feral wolf. I know because I've seen that particular one before. Years ago, I watched it fight a Gaggolang. It won the fight by shredding the Gaggolang into thousands of pieces with its long, razor-sharp teeth. Once it got a good grip on the Gaggolang, it began shaking as if it were having a tremor and yelling, 'Where's the crown?' before bursting the Gaggolang apart like fireworks. Sparks and flashing flames were flying everywhere and the Gaggolang was bellowing like a banshee. Then, the sparks of fire became so intense those of us watching had to run or be burned alive! This search for the crown has been going on forever, but now it's getting more intense. It seems like the entire world can feel its closeness. The ice-dragon is bringing it close to tempt the thieves in the hope that he finds Aunt Anna B's killer. It's close to being given to the rightful owner, but the dead are trying their best to steal it."

Lily and Ophelia stood silently staring at Bob for a few seconds.

"I don't understand how you know all this information, Bob" Ophelia whispered.

Bob did not reply.

"Well, let's go home," Lily said, breaking the awkward silence.

The three of them took off running. They passed the cemetery gate and were only a few minutes from the mansion when Lily stopped.

"Wait," Lily whispered. "Let's go down to the river and see if *The Sea's Shadow* makes and appearance. It's foggy, and I can't hear the river, so it must be calm. What do you think?"

Ophelia and Bob looked at Lily for a few seconds before nodding their heads in agreement.

8

The Sea's Shadow

Taking off their shoes, the three of them ran quietly past the house, being careful not to alert the adults. As they raced past the dark kitchen window, Lily thought she saw, just for a second, Mr. Kulicki's face staring at her. She wasn't sure, though – if he was there, he wasn't anymore. Her heart skipped a beat.

Bob was running faster than Lily and Ophelia. He ran to Main Street and was already reaching Waterfront street before the two of them could turn the corner onto Main. Realizing how far ahead he was, he stopped beneath the lamppost at the corner of Waterfront and waited for them to catch up.

"Dang, Bob," Ophelia said quietly, gasping for breath. "Don't run so fast."

They slowed down to catch their breath, walking slowly along Waterfront Street. Lily was glad they were all still dressed in black from the funeral, because she could feel restless shadows lurking around her. Something felt evil. Except for one small, lit window on the third floor of an old port mansion, every home on the narrow, deserted street was dark and deathly quiet. Wisps of pale mist blew gently from the river across their path and swirled into little eddies, pushing its way towards Main

Street. Restless tension thickened in the air as they continued to walk. She noticed the hair on her arms was standing straight up. In her peripheral vision, she thought she saw a shadow slip from one hiding place to another. She was confident they were being watched, but she did not know who was lurking about watching them.

As they grew closer to the river, the fog thickened, covering their shoes; it seemed to be trying to climb up to their knees. The solitary lit window on the port mansion cut its light out and the fog continued to climb. Lily noticed the eerie but beautiful swirling patterns it made around some of the lampposts. Lily was listening intently for any noise around them; in the hopes of hearing their followers. She could hear nothing except their bare feet slipping against the cobblestone street, and the sound of her own breathing.

An owl called out briefly in the distance.

They passed by a long-abandoned house on their right. The windows were boarded shut haphazardly; if it were light outside, she may have been able to see inside through the gaps in the boards. A gaping hole stood where the front door used to.

Thud.

The three of them jumped out of their skin, but stifled their screams. Automatically looking to the source of the noise, they noticed the breeze had slapped a broken shutter against the side of the old house. It was swaying back and forth, hanging by a single nail.

"Goodness gracious," Ophelia whispered quietly.

Lily glanced at the open door. Along the edge of the frame, hidden by shadow, was a man's leg. She saw his bare foot, and part of his pant leg. Her heartbeat grew fast and strong. Fear, curiosity and dread filled her very soul. Continuing to stare

148

at the shadow, she could make out fingertips grasping the rotting doorframe. Then she realized he was looking back at her. His face was barely visible in the darkness, under a hat pulled low. His cold eyes were staring straight at her, but he did not move.

Swallowing hard, Lily touched both Bob and Ophelia's arms and motioned towards the door opening. Ophelia's face turned pale. Bob grabbed both of their arms and tugged on them, indicating they should move faster. Trying their best to run quietly, the three of them quickly headed for the river's edge.

There in a patch of river grass, they put their shoes back on to avoid stepping on snakes. Lily looked back to see if they were being followed. They weren't. They hid inside the tall river grass hoping to catch a glimpse of *The Sea's Shadow*.

There they waited for maybe half an hour in silence. Eventually there came a sound of many oars dipping softly in and out of the water. Pushing aside the river grass, they crept silently to the river's edge. Hovering on the very top of the river water, came *The Sea's Shadow*, so close they would be able to touch it as it passed in front of them. It was scarcely about a half mile upriver from them.

They froze, transfixed with awe. What a magnificent, ghostly vessel it was, almost sixty feet in length, slender and sleek, built shallowly so as to skim the waters smoothly. It was as white as snow and as transparent as the fog it was sailing through. It slipped through the thick mist and glided the top of the waters easily. Its bow, the head of a fierce dragon, and its stern, a large barbed dragon tail, rose high above its body. Towering above the center of its body sat a single sail, unfurled and filled with the night air. Ornate, golden oarsmen's shields were latched over the side of the vessel, each next to its owner, placed there to be snatched up quickly if need be. The ghostly oarsmen rowed the ship slowly forward along the top of the water as fog swirled and curled in great wisps behind her. Lily could not make out the oarsmen's faces; they were hidden under some kind of murky shroud.

"Róa! róa!"

As the coxswain skeleton called out softly, twenty-five oarsmen on either side of the ship's trim body moved as one, each obeying his call. The coxswain and oarsmen were all snow-white skeletons. They all stared intently at the bank of the river, their hollow eye sockets searching. Closer and closer they came, until the ship was within reach of their fingers.

"Halt!" the coxswain called out.

With surprising speed and gentleness, the ship instantly came to a complete stop. The oarsmen maneuvered their oars to keep the ship in one place against the strong river currents. Suddenly, Lily could see the facial features of the oarsmen; the veils seemed to have melted from their faces.

Leaning their heads far back as possible, the three of them gawked, fascinated and spellbound at the vessel's beauty. Without warning, Ophelia reached out to touch the ship, as if in a trance. Bob snatched her hand away, shaking his head at her.

"Stop!" Bob whispered sharply. "If you touch her, she will take you onboard and never let you leave!"

Ophelia jumped back a few steps and turned pale as the moonlight. A rustle in the tall grasses to their left drew their attention. The figure of a man stepped out from the swamp grass and cattails. It was difficult to make out his face in the darkness, but Lily was sure it was the same man they had spotted in the old abandoned house.

"Ahhh," the fellow whispered as he walked closer and closer to the huge ghost vessel. "'Tis "*The Sea's Shadow*" viking ship! It has the crown onboard! I know it does!"

The three of them watched as the man drew near the vessel. When he reached the side of the ship, he stretched out his arms to climb aboard.

"No, no, no," Bob whispered loudly as he took a few steps towards the man.

Surprised to find a boy in the grass at this time of night, the man jerked his head around, drew his arms back, growled deep within his chest.

"Leave me be, boy! I'm getting that crown!"

He jumped towards the ship, grabbed the rim of a shield, and with a grunt, began to pull himself up and over the white, shimmering railing. Before he could swing his legs up and over, he was snatched by an unseen power, flung into the hull of the vessel. Looking through the transparent hull the three of them witnessed a look of pure terror come across the man's face, for there lying on the floor of the hull was the remains of a Gaggalong! Suddenly there was an explosion unlike any the three of them had heard before and the sky above the ship was filled with leaping tongues of fire so hot the three of them could feel the heat on their faces. Glittering sparks exploded in every direction, causing them to jump down into the cattails. Peeking through the thick grasses they watched as the screams of the man in the hull echoed across the delta and he slowly faded away into oblivion. Ice-blue sparks lingered above the vessel when out of the night came the cry of a dragon in flight. Then suddenly there before them, hovering high above the ship, was the ice dragon they had seen at Dragon's mountain. The glittering chain and shimmering gold crown were still dangling from its massive neck.

In one swift motion, the dragon swooped down and sat in the belly of the ship, hanging its head to the floor to rest. Neither the coxswain or the oarsmen seemed to realize that a dragon's ghost had just boarded their ship.

"Róa! Róa!"

Smooth and synchronized, the oarsmen moved the vessel further down the edge of the riverbank. Lily, Bob and Ophelia sat fascinated in the cattails as the massive Viking ship glided slowly into the dense fog and vanished, leaving no trace that it had ever been there on the shores of the Mississippi river.

9

Apparitions

Scrambling silently from the tall grass, Lily, Ophelia and Bob raced onto Waterfront Street. At the corner of Waterfront and Main, they once again stopped beneath the fading streetlamp to catch their breath.

"Have you seen her before, Bob?" Ophelia asked between gasps of breath.

"Nope," Bob answered. "And I've gone down there many times trying to spot her. I even sat in the top of a tree once, thinking maybe I could catch her unaware."

Lily sat on the ground under the lamppost, looking at Bob curiously.

"In the top of a tree?"

"Yeah," Bob replied, also sitting. "I figured if I was up high enough, maybe she wouldn't notice. But I never did see her until tonight."

"I think it's an apparition," Lily whispered softly. "It shows up and does the exact same thing every time it appears! Well, maybe not the part where the man blew up, but the coxswain and the oarsmen didn't seem to notice. Even when the dragon appeared and sat inside the ship, they didn't change expressions or anything! What do you think?"

"I think you're right," Bob said.

Ophelia tapped her finger against the lamppost. "Yeah, I think so too," she muttered as she took a seat. Bob looked around the street curiously.

"Let's go on home and sit on the front steps. This place gives me the willies," he said.

Jumping up, the three of them hurried down Main Street until they got to the front of the old mansion where they then ran up the thirty steps and took a seat on the top step so they could see all the way to the Mississippi River. They sat in silence for a few moments. They were starting to feel fatigue set in from the long day.

"I remember an apparition in Granny Zephyr's house when I was younger that scared the heebie-jeebies out of me," Lily whispered softly. "Great-Granny Zephyr lived way over in Kentucky, deep in a valley of the Great Smokey Mountains. Well, before she passed on, I got to stay with her for a whole summer, and one night, I was all alone on her front porch and I spied something white coming up to her house. Well, I screamed out, and Granny came running as the white figure disappeared in an instant. She told me it was just an apparition, and 'apparitions don't do anything a'tall, except show up every so often looking for what they loved while they were alive'."

Lily tried her best to imitate Granny's old, shaky voice as she talked. Ophelia chuckled. Lily continued in her normal voice.

"Granny told me that way back in the late 1600's, a young woman named Sari Jane died in Granny's house giving birth to a baby boy, so she was sure it was that same young woman coming back to find her little baby. Well, a few nights later, me and Granny saw the apparition again while we were sitting on the front porch with all the lights off so we could see all the

154

fireflies flashing and blinking. Suddenly, there she came, floating up the road to Granny's house as if she had just come from town. She was tall and slender, and her hair hung way down her back almost to the back of her knees! It wasn't foggy that night like it usually was, so we could see her pretty clearly. She was all white, just like the Viking ship tonight. Her dress was blowing really slow-like around her body.

"Granny had seen her before and said she did the same thing every time she came to the house. She would walk up the porch steps, go right on through the door and look in each room of Granny's house, then sigh, walk back out and melt into the night. But that night it was a bit different. That night, Sari June stopped at the top of Granny's steps, turned her face towards us and smiled before entering the house. When she came back out, looked at me and Granny and nodded her head as if to say 'thank you', then faded into the night.

Sari June came to Granny's house once a week for the that entire summer. Then late one fog-filled evening, an old, old woman named Maudie Blue Harper came to Granny's door, rapped sharply. then opened the door and walked right inside as if she owned the place. I guess Mrs. Maudie Blue lived alone, deep in a holler one away from Granny. Well anyway, she took a seat in Granny's rocker and said she wanted some hot tea. So, Granny, who was still getting up to answer the door, got her wrap on and fixed some hot tea and the three of us sat at the eating table.

"After taking forever to drink her tea, she told us the spirit of Sari June wouldn't be coming back a'tall now, 'cuz she finally found her baby boy. Maudie Blue had seen Sari June's apparition on the road and somehow guided her to the graveyard where her baby boy had been laid to rest. Turns out the baby had passed on three hours after his mama passed on. Sari June's apparition wept like a baby when she first saw his little headstone, and then she looked at Maudie Blue, smiled, and melted away into the night with the spirit of a tiny baby in her arms."

Ophelia stared at Lily for a minute before saying anything

"Was that the summer I went down to Vacherie with my mama?"

"Yep, it was. Why?"

"Well, what do you know!" Ophelia said with wide-eyed unbelief. "Me and Mama saw some apparitions down there by New Orleans in Vacherie when we stayed with my great, great Pappy Ballard Dubois for a while. He's not really my blood kin, but I guess he was like a Grandpa to Mama, because she always calls him Pappy. He lived way out in the bayou of south Louisiana. He *said* he was married to an old Cajun woman named Sophianna Marcella Antoinette. Now Mama didn't think they was actually married, because every night she would leave and go to another man's house, claiming she was being paid to take care of the old fella. Well, one Monday morning she didn't show up at the usual time, so Mama got to looking around the house, trying to find an address where she could find her. Low-and-behold, she found a bunch of voodoo things shoved way back in a closet, and some papers showing Sophianna was married to a fella named Baumgart DuBois, who was Pappy Dubois' cousin!

"So, she calmly started in asking Pappy Dubois about his cousin Baumgart, and Pappy told Mama that Baumgart lived just a couple miles down the road at the other end of Vacherie. When Mama asked Pappy if Baumgart was the man Sophianna was taking care of during the night, Pappy told her that, indeed, he was.

"Well, Mama and I got in the buggy and took off down the road to find Baumgart's house. When we found it, we walked up to the door and gave it a good solid knock, but no one answered so Mama turned the knob and we quietly walked inside. It was an old, one-room cabin with a bed on one side and a cook stove on the other. Well, there in the bed together were the apparitions of Baumgart and Sophianna, who vanished into thin air as soon as they got a look at us. Well, me and Mama looked everywhere for their bodies, thinking maybe they had somehow died during the night. We didn't find anything.

"So, we got back into the buggy and started back towards Pappy Dubois' house just as a storm began pouring rain down upon us. Mama spotted a big house on stilts sitting back off the road a bit, so she pulled the buggy up to the front door and we jumped down and raced up the steps to the long, covered porch. There we were met by a big, husky, kind-looking man who opened the door and invited us inside. Well, Mama said we were sorry to bother him but we were wondering if he knew where Mr. Baumgart Dubois and Sophianna Dubois happened to be. The man looked at us kindly strange, and said, 'Yes, ma'am, I know where they are'.

He just stood there looking at us silently for a minute or two before Mama asked him where might they be. He turned his head kind of cock-eyed as if he didn't believe she was looking for them. Then he said, 'They're still in prison, as far as I know, unless they've escaped.'"

"Well, Mama's eyes got big as saucers. She asked why they were in prison, and he said that Sophianna had murdered her first husband, Ballard Dubois, before running off to New Orleans with Baumgart."

Lily stared open-mouthed at Ophelia. "So what did you and your mama do?"

"Mama told him Ballard had been like a grandpa to her, and she asked him if he knew what happened to his body. The man looked sad, and said he had been buried in the chapel cemetery of St. Bernard in Vacherie. Then the man asked us to have a seat on the porch, so we did, and he told us the story of Baumgart, Sophianna and Pappy Ballard. He said Sophianna had been married to Pappy for a few years when she met Baumgart. I guess Baumgart took a liking to her and she started in seeing Baumgart behind Pappy Ballard's back. Well, the fella told us how pretty soon, Baumgart started talking nonsense about getting Sophianna away from Ballard so they could find a golden crown. But he needed Sophianna and her brother Booger to help him do the deed.'

Lily and Bob frowned and stared at Ophelia.

"Are you sure that's what the fella said?" Lily asked as she scratched her elbow. She had a habit of scratching her elbow when she was nervous. "That's impossible."

"That's what he said," Ophelia replied as she shook her head, raising her shaky right hand. "I swear on the grave of my Granny Gertie. He said Baumgart and Sophianna wanted to find a gold, polished crown."

"Well, what happened after that?" Bob asked, frowning.

"Well, the fella said they did away with Pappy Ballard then buried him in a shallow grave next to his barn."

"No, I mean what did you and your mama do?"

"Oh, we went back to our buggy, and when we got in, we both turned back to tell the fella thank you, but he was gone. In his place stood a hunched over, shriveled up old man, kindly see-through like those Viking ghosts. He had a shriveled-up mouth as if he had lost all his teeth. The beautiful house had vanished and now looked abandoned, as if no one had lived there for years and years. The windows were broken out and the door was hanging on its rope hinges. The old man gave us a friendly wave and a toothless smile. Then Mama pulled the buggy out of the path but I turned and kept looking back at the old man. He kept on waving and smiling so I waved back and then, in the upstairs window I saw an old woman staring back at me. I think she was an apparition too.

"Mama took us back to Pappy Ballard's house quickly, where we walked cautiously inside and found the house empty and hollow-sounding as if we and Pappy Ballard had never been there. The back-screen door was slapping against its frame and leaves were blowing in through the open windows. Our carpet bags were sitting in the middle of the parlor and it looked as if all our things had been packed up to go. I remember hanging tight onto Mama's hand as we walked through the house. Pappy Ballard's bed was made up and on the bureau was an envelope with Mama's name written on the front. Mama picked up the envelope and stuck it in her front pocket then we both went out and climbed into the buggy before mama opened the envelope.

"It was a letter in Pappy Ballard's handwriting. Mama read it quietly to me since I didn't know how to read as of yet. Pappy Ballard told Mama everything in the house and all the property now belonged to her, and that he had lingered around waiting for Mama to come down so he could see her one last time. Inside the envelope was also all the money Pappy possessed. It wasn't much, Mama said, but it was precious to her.

When Mama stopped reading, she looked at me and said, 'This is the last we will ever talk about what we have seen and heard today. Put it out of your mind and never think on it again.'

"Mama didn't say one more word," Ophelia continued, "and neither did I, all the way to Vacherie. She drove us to the town stable where she handed the owner of the stables the reins to the horse and buggy. She told him who she was, and that Pappy Ballard had always spoke highly of him, and since she was his sole relative, she knew Mr. Dubois would want him to have them. The stable owner, Mr. Pierre, looked a bit surprised and tried to pay her for them, but she refused and told him we were in a hurry to catch the next train to New Orleans. So, the fella thanked her and stood there watching us. Mama looked down at me and said it was Mr. Pierre's lucky day.

"From there, we walked to the Sheriff's office and Mama asked the sheriff if he knew what had happed to Baumgart and Sophianna Dubois. The Sheriff told us that, sure enough, they had been sent to the Cajun prison for doing away with Ballard Dubois, but both had died of the Yellow Fever less than 6 months ago. Mama asked him why she had not been notified of Pappy Ballard's death, and he told her Sophianna told him that Mama and all her family had moved to France and that she was going to send a wire to notify us. Well, Mama thanked him then we hurried out to the train depot where Mama bought us tickets to New Orleans where we would catch the train back home. And that was the last I thought of what happened down in voodoo country until just now."

Lily and Ophelia looked at Bob, who was staring out across the Mississippi with a glazed look on his face.

"Bob...Bob!" Lily poked him in the elbow to get his attention, "have you ever seen any apparitions?"

Bob sat there silently for a few minutes before answering.

"Yeah, but you really don't want to hear about them. They weren't nice or polite or anything like the apparitions y'all saw."

"Yes, we do," Lily and Ophelia said in unison.

For a very long minute looked at them with a solemn face then whispered quietly, "No you don't...not really."

10

Father Fritz

The three of them were sitting quietly staring across the Mississippi river when a small lantern light could be seen coming up from the road to the south of them. Still not saying a word, the three watched uneasily until the shadowy figure of Father Fritz emerged out of the darkness in his long white nightshirt and a night cap dangling from the side of his head. His feet were bare, as he shuffled slowly towards them carrying the small, swinging lantern. Puzzled, they watched him make his way slowly up the thirty steps, plopped down beside Lily and sighed deeply.

"Father Fritz," Lily finally asked in a soft whisper, "What are you doing out in this foggy night?"

He sat in silence for a moment, catching his breath.

"I was worried about your young foolish souls," he answered. "I knew you had gone down to the riverfront looking for the *Sea's Shadow*, so I decided to come have a check and make sure you were all okay."

Bob, Lily and Ophelia continued staring at the old priest until they realized they were being rude.

"Well, we did see her, and it was exciting for sure!" Ophelia exclaimed, once again looking out at the slow-moving river. "We were telling each other about the apparitions we have seen. Have you ever seen an apparition Father Fritz?"

"Ahhhh, yes," he replied softly. "I have seen many apparitions in my years upon this earth. Some you shall never hear about from me, but some were not so bad a'tall."

He looked at Lily.

"Shall I tell you of them?"

"Yes!" Lily whispered emphatically as shivers ran up and down her spine, knowing they would be frightening tales.

Bob sat tense and quiet; not saying a word - just staring intently at Father Fritz.

"Okay," Father Fritz replied. "I have told Bob this tale many years ago – haven't I, Bob? 'Tis a good one isn't it, lad? Not too frightening but not too dull."

Bob seemed to relax a bit as he looked at the old priest and nodded. "It is unusual, Father Fritz, quite unusual."

Something was not quite right with Bob. Lily could feel it in her bones.

"Now, I'm only telling you this because I know the two of you will not doubt my telling since you were able to see the lovely spirit of Annabelle Bloome at her own funeral – with all her silly antics and shenanigans." He smiled at them then gazed across the river as he continued.

"I was born many, many moons ago, as my Kickapoo friends say, further back than you can ever imagine." He paused for a moment. It was silent.

"T'was during the darkest days of the Dark Ages in the year 527 when I appeared on earth," he began in a whispery voice. "T'was a time when spirits and strange creatures plagued the lands of Europe, roaming throughout the forests and pillaging the small villages. Back when apparitions were abundant and a soul never new if the person next to them was created by God or by evil.

"On the day I made my entrance into that forsaken land it was as if mankind had embraced evil until God himself turned his face from this wicked world. In a tiny village called Merkishino, deep in the Ural Mountains of Russia, I slipped quietly into a world where there was no sun and no love for neighbors among the poor, wretched souls that were always stealing, scrapping and begging for food and shelter.

"On that day the skies were grayer than most; or so I was told. I cried loudly for my mother, but there were no kind words or anyone to pick up and cuddle my tiny body as I lay wrapped in dirty rags. My papa sat sobbing at the bedside of my mother as she exhaled her last exhausted breath after the birthing. As the life ebbed out of her, my papa slipped slowly to the floor and his spirit rose to meet Mother's, as he too left me alone. The old woman who had been in the house to help with the birthing picked up her bag, hurried out, shutting the door tight behind her. and leaving me to the elements of the wild and the blistering-cold mountain winds. My tiny body lay quivering and hungry for two days before a traveling tinker-man, by the name of Mikhail, came along and heard my feeble, weak cries. He rushed into the hut thinking to help my mother but found me alone with my parents' lifeless bodies. He kindly buried my Mom and Papa, wrapped me in a warm Russian blanket, and went about the village in search of someone who would take me in. The old woman who had helped mother give birth told him to get rid of me because the spirits told her I was no good and would bring a curse on the village."

Father Fritz chuckled deep within his chest as he said, "As if the village had not been cursed already."

"She told him she could hear me crying throughout the night and was glad he had found me since she was thinking of taking me into the forest and leaving me for the wolves. Not one soul in the village came to my rescue, so Mikhail himself carried me back to the tiny hut where I was born, gave me milk from his lone milk cow tied behind his cart, built a fire to keep both of us warm as we spent the night there in that forgotten village. The next day he took me with him as he rode out, bundling me tightly in his blanket and put me into a wooden box under the cart bench so I would be out of the bitter cold and intense winds of winter. He guided his horse-drawn cart through the howling artic winds and blowing snow of the rough and rutted roads until we reached the bottom of a valley where he knew of a place to find shelter for both of us. His lone milk cow from which he sold milk along the way was the only thing that kept me alive through those first years of my life, so he told me.

"By the time I was ten years of age I knew the tinker business as well as old Mikhail. He was an old man when he found me, and when I was about thirteen, he got too old to drive his cart, so I drove it for him."

Father Fritz stopped talked and smiled.

"We had a jolly good time, me and old Mikhail, as he would say in his English accent, going up and down those mountains selling his wares. He taught me to speak and write Russian and English along with how to read every spot of writing I could find. He had sailed on the great oceans and tramped across vast continents of open lands of every culture."

Once again, he looked at the three of them sitting next to him.

"It was a time of great ignorance and oppression. In an entire village maybe one person could read or write and usually that would be the priest who journeyed from village to village. At each stop along our way Mikhail would begin his sales by standing on the seat of the cart and telling elaborate tales of dragons and terrifying forest dwellers who slip into houses without being seen and do evil until those living in the houses lifted their Bibles and frightened them away. Then Mikhail would bring out his goods, which always contained Bibles, and using his kind, gentle voice he would sell all his Bibles - even though not a single soul could read - and the rest of his other goods for less than a penny in today's society. Many a time we gave away more than we sold to help those with no means of which to pay. When we left every little village, he would say to me, as he had the village before, 'Son, I am putting half our coins in this box beneath our bench. It is for you when I am too old to make these journeys and we must stop our travels to find a place for me to live or for you to continue traveling alone if you choose.'

"We guided that horse through snow up to our knees and ice so thick I could barely break it up to get to water. One morning when I was 15 years, old Mikhail did not wake up. The frost had covered the fall grasses and the cold, polar air from Finland blew down upon us, seeping through the cracks in our cloth cart walls. We were close to the small village of Veliky, not far from where Saint Petersburg is today. I sat on the bench for quite a while in our tiny cramped cart and pondered on what to do, then I picked up a shovel and ax and buried him - my father and my best friend. As a marker I pulled the cart over his grave, took off its high wheels and lowered it over the earth so no animal could get to him and left his belongings inside. I figured if anyone came along and stole them it would be between them and God.

"Picking up the small box of coins and what else I thought I needed, I tied it into a bundle, strapped it on my back, put my bow and arrows across my shoulder and rode out on that old horse into Veliky where I gave him to a struggling family in exchange for a meal of simple gruel and cold water. The lady of the house insisted I spend the night and packed me a bit of bread for my journey the next day.

"Well, early the next morning after sleeping on the floor of the shanty - which housed seven people - I slipped out the door before daybreak and headed into the mountains. I trudged through the Urals, going south in hopes of making it to Kyiv and warmer weather where I could go to work on a ship which may take me down to the Black Sea. From there I hoped to begin my travels just as my Mikhail had done in the past. He had told me

166

many stories of all those places he had been and I wanted to see every one of them for myself.

"From all the days Mikhail and I had traveled through that desolate land I learned every turn in the roads, or so I thought, but along about noontime I realized the sun was on the wrong side of me, so with a sigh I turned and trekked back until the now setting sun was on the right side of my face. The cold winds started up again in blustery gusts, lashing around the forest trees until I was sure they would topple, so I stopped and wrapped one of my wool blankets around myself and pulled my ushanka under my chin. About three o'clock in the afternoon, or there abouts, I spotted a dirt and wood shanty up on the side of the mountain I was circling, so I began climbing my way up. It was further than I expected it to be, but finally I made it right before the sun set."

Father Fritz hesitated for a few seconds. Lily glanced at Ophelia, who was staring white-faced at Father Fritz.

"Are you a ghost?" Ophelia asked in a soft, quivering voice.

"No," Father Fritz replied hesitantly. He cocked his head to one side and whispered, "Not really."

Bob coughed and gave Ophelia a nudge in the arm.

"Then what happened?" Bob asked as he poked Ophelia sharply in the side again as if signaling her not to ask questions.

"I'll tell you in a bit, child," Father Fritz smiled at Ophelia. "Hold on and let me tell you about the apparitions."

"Well," he continued after reaching around Lily and patting Ophelia on the arm in a comforting gesture.

"By the time I reached that run-down little half-sod shanty, I was hungry and damp from the fog coming into the mountain and I didn't care if the place was packed with wolves, I was going inside to start me a small fire, roast some late fall cabbage and a couple rutabaga then lie down for the night. Cautiously I pushed open the door a bit and immediately the musty smell of an uninhabited dwelling enveloped me, then swooped out the door like that of a spirit escaping a cage. Bones, leaves and broken furniture lay scattered within the small abode but I didn't care; all I could think of was eating then laying down. Brushing the dead, dried leaves into a small pile and lying a few dried twigs on top I managed to get myself a small but sustainable fire going. It wasn't long before the smells of roasting cabbage and rutabaga filled the shanty with its warmth.

"To my hungry stomach, that was a feast fit for a king." Father Fritz smiled and rubbed his stomach as if the tastes were still with him.

"Then," he said as he looked at the three of them and lowered his voice, "I brushed aside the animal bones and leaves as best I could and made myself a nice place to roll into my thick warm blanket and lay my head for the night as the little fire grew smaller and smaller."

"Long about midnight, or so it seemed, I woke with a start but didn't move a muscle, sensing that my body had detected something amiss. As old Mikhail had taught me to do when surprised by an unknown spirit, I lay perfectly still and barely opened my eyes. My inner soul told me I was no longer alone in that tiny shanty, and whether it be human, animal or spirit I did not know. Opening up my eyes just a wee bit more, I peered around that room trying to focus in the blackness. Then I saw it. My heart began thundering in my chest and the palms of my hands turned sweaty, for there in the upper corner of the room; staring back at me were the eyes of an unknown creature. Till this very day shivers race up and down my spine when I look back on it, and the hair on my arms stand straight up when I remember those ghostly eyes slowly blinking back at me. They were narrow, slanted ice-blue eyes staring directly at me and glowing bright in the bitter, cold darkness of that little shanty!

"To my horror, I watched as its body became visible. A long, tall apparition gradually formed and occupied that dark, shadowy corner from top to bottom. Its head was so high it had to bend its neck down or it would have popped through the roof and its arms reached almost to the ground and its legs were longer than its entire upper body. There was no flesh upon its bones, only a shadowy skeleton. Suddenly it lunged to the floor and frantically began pushing away the bones and leaves as if desperately searching for something of value. When it got to the place where I lay, its hands went right through me as if I were not even there and it began sweeping the ground beneath me with its skeletal bone hands. My poor body shook and shivered as the cold from the creature's body pushed and shoved within me. It gave a sharp jerk on something under me and instantly I was thrown into the middle of the shanty floor by a hidden trap door as the creature ripped it open and sent me flying. Out from the hole in the floor the being pulled forth a long, glistening sword with jewels shining in the darkness as if lit by an unseen fire.

"Then, I heard a rustle outside the shanty and in through the door, without even opening it, burst another apparition. It was the apparition of a Viking dressed in full Viking-warrior armor, riding a huge stallion which, itself was covered in armor and jewels. Then, another came in behind that one, then another and another until that little shanty was packed to the roof with apparitions of Vikings and their horses! The biggest, fiercest, apparition bellowed out, 'Charge!' and with the sound of thundering horse hooves and the clicking of swords, the Vikings charged the skeleton. Instantly the tiny shanty became as big as a wide-open field as the single skeleton and the many Vikings began battle. I watched in horror as right before my face the Vikings leapt from their horses and jumped upon the shadowy bone apparition and a wild furious melee commenced as the bones of the shadowy skeleton flew in many directions. Then, like magic the entire army of Vikings, me and the bones of the skeleton were no longer on an open field but were back inside the tiny shanty. I scooted myself as far back against a wall as possible then suddenly the earth began to tremble and quake furiously. I watched the walls shaking and bending and right then and there I knew those flimsy walls were gonna burst right apart at the seams and fall in upon me. I could feel the air swishing as those apparitions continued swinging their swords as I was being kicked back and forth under their feet! I didn't know how they were doing it, being apparitions, but they were. Frantically

I tried scrambling for the door but a big burly Viking was blocking my way. Now, I couldn't figure out if any of those apparitions could actually see me, but that big ugly one could. He looked down at me as I looked up at him and a wicked smirk came across his huge, ugly, face as he kicked his leg backwards and with the sole of his boot knocked the door wide open. Then he gave me a boot in the behind and out the door I flew where all the apparition horses were prancing and dancing about. I landed in the knee-high snow then rolled over and over as I listened to the big fella laughing.

"By that time the earth had stopped shaking and trembling, so I scrambled up from a snow bank which had stopped me from rolling right on down the mountain, then scurried to one side of the shanty, kicked a wall board out, then wiggled my way inside to my bundle of things, grabbed them up, then wiggled my way back out through the same hole and started off down the mountainside. Looking back for a minute, I could see flashes and sparks shooting out of every opening in that little shack. Then, suddenly, *BOOM!* Its walls fell outward and the entire roof came crashing down on top of all those apparitions, and like magic, every last one of them - including the bone apparition, who was now in one skeletal body again - swooped out and vanished into the night. It was the strangest thing I had ever seen in my 15 years. There must have been fifty or more apparitions crammed inside that tiny shack but in a matter of seconds they were gone. So, I stood there in the darkness looking up at that tiny shanty and listening to the wolves' howl. Shaking my head in disbelief, I figured I might as well squeeze myself under the fallen roof for a bit of shelter from the hungry wolves and wait until morning to leave, and so I did.

"I slept through the rest of the night as sound as a dead dog. In the morning, the snow was up to my waist and I knew I wasn't going anywhere. Well, the day wore on and long about noontime the sun came out and began melting the snow, but dusk was also coming on before it melted enough for me to move on, and I sure didn't want to be out in the wilderness when full night came so I decided to stay put. When dusk came to the mountain, I crawled back under that fallen roof and lay there looking out at the world until I fell sound asleep, then once again around midnight, or so, my eyes popped open and there with me under that fallen roof was the same bone ghost with them big slanted ice-blue eyes. And, once again he blinked a couple times, dropped to his knees and, the same as the night before, began brushing under those boards as if to find something. Well, I knew what was going to happen next so I scooted as far back as I could and waited for the Viking apparitions to burst in through the door and sure enough, there they were under that roof with the two of us. Suddenly, all those boards popped back into place, the roof went up where it was supposed to be and they began fighting like heathens. So, again I scrambled to the door and waited for the big galoot of a Viking to give me a kick in the britches and sure enough, he obliged and as was the night before, I went rolling into that big snow bank again. But this time I had grabbed up my bundle and blanket before I was booted out the door."

Father Fritz gave out a loud laugh.

"Well, I was pretty sure the roof was gonna fall in on itself again, so I waited and sure enough, it fell. Right on top of all those fighting apparitions and, once again, they vanished into thin air. So, with a sigh, I crawled under the fallen roof just as I had done the previous night."

Father Fritz looked at Lily for a second or two before nodding his head and saying, "Your Granny Zephyr was right, Lily. Apparitions repeat the same thing night after night after night.

"I no more than got myself all settled into my thick Russian blanket, away from that miserable wind coming down from the Artic when I heard a roar like nothing I had heard before. I squirmed and wiggled from beneath that old fallen roof and there before me were more dragons than I could ever imagine! The

171

sky was filled with the critters; big ones, small ones from the Ural Mountain to giant red dragons from Mongolia as well as dragon apparitions, dragon skeletons and every other kind of dragon creature you can imagine. There were even tiny little dragons scurrying around my ankles blowing out tiny clouds of smoke. Thank goodness they hadn't learned how to blow flames! Anyway, they were fighting about something; I never did figure out what it was, but it was a sight to behold! The biggest one of all was an ice-blue dragon, and he was a monster. He wore a shiny, thick, gold chain around his neck and dangling from it a glistening crown swayed and flipped around as he flew erratically through the sky. Can you believe that?"

Bob poked Lily in the side and Lily poked Ophelia then all three of them stared at Father Fritz.

"Was the big ice-blue dragon fighting like all the rest?" Lily asked softly.

"No, not at all, he was dipping and diving in the sky like crazy and all the other dragons were chasing him as they bit and shoved and wrestled with each other all at the same time. The smaller mountain dragons were throwing out flames one right after the other while the larger ones were pushing and biting each other. I stood mesmerized as I watched the fight in the night sky. The stars were bright and the moon seemed to bounce its beams off the big ice-dragon. Off to his right soared a green dragon with fiery red eyes and horns starting at the top of his head going all the way down to the start of its barbed tail. It was swooping and flipping over and over as it tried maneuvering itself closer to the ice-dragon. But, none of those dragons could catch that big fella even though it looked like he was putting very little effort into staying ahead of them.

"Then, suddenly, as if slamming on their brakes, every dragon in the sky skidded to a stop, looked down at me then with a loud *swoop* landed right smack in front of me as their huge wings created a sound like thunder echoing through the mountain.

"I was both terrified and stunned as I stood staring with open-mouth wonder at the sight before me. Then, slowly one by one, they began swaying back and forth from one foot to the other and making this weird *awwkkk, awwkkk* sound. Then, little by little, step by step, the whole group - which seemed to cover the entire side of the mountain - advanced towards me. Cautiously I stepped back a bit, keeping my eyes locked with theirs, knowing full well if I turned to run, they would be upon me within seconds. Then, *SWOOP* "

Father Fritz made a swooping motion with his arms. "As quick as a firefly flash the green dragon pounced upon me, flung me up between the horns on his neck and off we flew into the night sky high above the mountains. We went east towards the rising sun in the horizon. After my initial shock, I sat up, took me a look-see and feared he was taking me to his den to have me for breakfast!"

Bob gave out a little snort of laughter.

"We were so high I could see all the way to the Atlantic Ocean," Father Fritz continued, "well, not really but it sure seemed like it at the time."

Lily looked at Ophelia and Ophelia looked back at Lily with eyes wide.

"Father Fritz," Lily whispered softly, "by any chance was his name Bijou?"

Father Fritz did a quick little scoot around and turned to stare at Lily and Ophelia. Raising his eyebrows in surprise, he said with quiet surprise, "Indeed it was! And how did the two of you know that?"

Bob, who had been sitting silently on the top step piped up and said, "Because they met him inside the house a few nights ago, and he also gave them a ride down from the side of Dragon's mountain."

"Dragon's mountain? What were the two of you doing on the side of Dragon's mountain?"

173

"Nothing much," Lily whispered softly. "Please, Father Fritz, continue your story."

He frowned quietly.

"Okay, but we will talk another time about Dragon's mountain and the dangers there."

He turned back around to look out over the river before beginning again.

"That green dragon soared and swooped around those Ural's like an eagle with me hanging onto his horns for dear life. After a while I grew sleepy and wrapped myself around one of his horns and fell sound asleep. The next thing I knew he came to a mind-jarring stop as he skidded onto solid ground where he himself tumbled head over heels a few times. He had tossed me off with his first tumble. 'Sorry,' he said to me in his gravelly voice. 'I'm not a very good lander.' Shaking myself, I looked up and low-and-behold we were on the side of a mountain but it wasn't cold and dreary like the Urals. It was a bright, sunny day and the mountains were full of green trees, birds and flowers. That crazy dragon lowered his head and looked at me closely. 'You okay?' he asked. I nodded, then off he flew, leaving me alone in this unknown wilderness. I stood there stunned for a bit then got up and began walking down the mountain. I hadn't taken but five steps when he reappeared, sat down on his haunches in front of me in the clearing where he had dumped. He sat there like a pup sitting on his haunches for a bit before saying anything a'tall.

"'Come back here for a few,' he then said in a gravelly voice. 'You are a Carmray. What were you doing in the mountains of Russia? Hunting for the crown?'

"I told him my name was Finees Fritzlin and that I had no idea who the Carmray's were and I had no idea what crown he was talking about. He looked at me with one of his fiery red eyes and frowned as he bent down to stare straight into my eyes with a hypnotic stare.

"'No! YOU are a Carmray. It's not your name, it's who you are,' he said. He sighed deeply then plopped down onto the ground and rolled onto his back with his back with his enormous belly protruding out and his feet sticking straight up in the air. His wide wings spread across the meadow.

"'I instructed that no-good Mikhail to tell you about yourself! He's a no-good bum and I'm tired of doing his duty for him,' he said with an angry tone.

"Immediately I jumped up, grabbed a pretty large tree branch up from the ground, walked over to the dragon and gave him a good solid smack on the end of his long snoot. 'Don't ever talk about my Mikhail like that again! He was my father and my friend,' I said.

"He roared as he put his front claws over his now bloody snoot. 'OUCH! Why did you do that? He *is* a no-good bum! He didn't do what he was supposed to do with you!'

"*SMACK*, I hit him again on the snoot."

"'*Stop it*!' he cried, but I said, 'I'll stop when you stop calling Mikhail a no-good bum!'

"'Well, he...' the dragon started, but I raised the branch again and he stopped in mid-sentence. He sighed loudly, then rolled onto his massive stomach with a groan.

"'You, my young friend, are a Carmray. Not a human, and not a spirit - but something in between. You could live for a very, very long time - or you could die any minute if you hit me with that branch again.'

"'What?' I asked him, 'What in the world are you talking about? Mikhail found me in the tiny hut where I was born."

"'So, he did, so he did,' he said back to me, scratching his chin with one of his long claws. 'But the fact is, he saw your spirit leaving your body as he stepped through the door of that hut so he reached up, snatched it from the air and flung it back into your body. So, now you are a Carmray.'"

Lily and Ophelia quietly inched a bit away from Father Fritz. Lily swallowed hard and kept on staring at Father Fritz as if he were from outer space - which he probably was! Ophelia was breathing in quick little gasps until Lily gave her a pinch on her arm so she wouldn't fall over in a faint.

"Well," Father Fritz casually continued speaking as if he had not just told them that he was some kind of foreign being, "Big Green told me his name was Bijou and that he lived deep within the mountain we were standing upon then he rolled onto his side, put his massive head in his front paw and told me about the mountain and how the crown was stashed there until the ice-dragon stole it and began flying around the galaxy showing it off to other dragons. He told me his job was to make sure I was kept safe since Mikhail had up and died on him. He never did tell me what kind of being Mikhail was, but after I heard Big Green's story, I reckoned Mikhail was a Carmray too. But, anyway, ever since then, down through the ages I have been a tinker and a gravedigger."

He stopped speaking and looked at them a bit sheepishly, and chuckled. "Also, a grave robber, a cobbler, a soldier in Constantine's army, a doctor in the American Revolutionary War, and now I am a Catholic priest which I shall stay until I die and I refuse to take any questions at all about this crown business."

With that said, he stood up, picked up his lantern and without another word slowly and with great care walked down the thirty some steps to the road leading back to the church parish. At the first lighted lamppost he turned slightly, raised his hand in the air, waved, then seemed to vanish into the misty fog tumbling slowly along the street.

"Well," Lily said as she looked at Ophelia and Bob with a frown, "that was weird. Did he just vanish or did the fog swallow him up?"

Neither Bob nor Ophelia answered. Rising from their seats on the top steps, the three of them peered into the dark night trying to catch a glimpse of Father Fritz, but not a soul could be seen on the deserted, shadowy road leading to the parish.

Out of the corner of her eyes, Lily caught the glimpse of a shadow at the opposite end of the long porch moving quickly from one giant flowering bush to another. Immediately grabbing Ophelia's arm, Lily pulled her - with Bob following close behind - through the large massive door of the house, turned around and slid the lock and swallowed the huge lump in her throat.

"What was that for?" Ophelia whispered so as to not awaken anyone.

"There was a shadow moving in the bushes at the other end of the porch."

"Maybe it was just the breeze."

"Maybe," Lily said quietly, but in her mind, she was sure the shadow had been Miss Josephine. Ophelia stared at her friend for a minute but said nothing.

"Come on," Lily said quietly, feeling uneasy. "Let's go to sleep and get up early tomorrow and do some exploring."

Bob stood quietly beside the massive door staring at the two girls until they disappeared up the stairs then quietly slid the lock on the door and stepped out into the night.

11

Creatures in the Night

Sprinting down the steps two at a time, Bob made it to the road in no time at all. He then raced towards Father Fritz' small house.

Looking out their bedroom window, Lily and Ophelia quite clearly saw Bob running for the parish, but he did not know they could see him.

"Look," Lily whispered, "that's Bob running towards the parish!"

Hand cranking the window open, the two of them leaned out and watched Bob as he sprinted down the dark, shadowy road.

"Wonder why?" Ophelia whispered almost to herself.

"I have no idea. Why would he be going to see Father Fritz? Maybe he's going someplace else."

"I don't know, Lily, but Bob has been a strange one since the first day we met. Right from the start, don't you think?"

"Well," Lily hesitated and thought for a minute. "Yeah. When I think about it, it is kind of strange. Come on, lets follow him."

Lily walked to the door, then hesitated before opening it.

"You know another thing I just thought of - it *is* strange why Otto never speaks to Bob. It's as if he totally ignores him. Have you noticed that?"

"I have," Ophelia said, "but I thought maybe it was just me. I wonder why?"

"I don't know," Lily muttered, shaking her head.

Easing the door open, they stepped quietly onto the long, shadowy front porch. Lily peered into the thick flower bushes at the end of the long porch and saw no moving shadows. Without a word, down the steep steps they flew until they reached the road leading south towards the tiny church parsonage. When they came within sight of the parish, they stopped running and slipped into the thick, dark trees surrounding the church, hoping to travel unseen.

Reaching the back of the tiny, parish house, they squatted low amongst some bushes. There, not far from them, was a small gathering of people around a little fire in a clearing not twenty feet into the and they seemed to be talking rapidly amongst themselves. The girls looked closer. It was Father Fritz, Brother Bartholomew, Brother Phillip, Bob, and a man that neither Lily or Ophelia had ever seen in Vicksburg. The stranger wore a black suit which was a little scruffy around the edges, but Lily could tell he was a gentleman, and his suit, at one time, had been quite handsomely made.

Lily had the feeling this man was kind; although she had no idea as to why.

Raising his weathered hand above his head, the unknown gentleman laughed and said something to the others which, in turn, made them all laugh loudly.

"Ah," Father Fritz spoke loudly enough that Lily and Ophelia could clearly hear his words, "Father Coydon, you are the right man to have around in these troubling days. Happiness always abounds with you. May God bless your kind soul."

"Oh, 'tis my Tillie who keeps me laughing even in my old age," Father Coydon replied with a chuckle. "Yes indeed, 'tis my Tillie."

Lily and Ophelia looked at each other, mouths dropped open in surprise.

"Did he say *Tillie*?" Lily mouthed to her friend.

"Yes!" Ophelia whispered back. "that's Tillie Brown's father, Mr. Brown. I kept thinking he looked kind of familiar, but it's too shadowy to really tell."

Lily looked again, this time a little harder. Father Coydon's hands were tanned and weathered as if he had worked years of long hours in the hot Mississippi sun. His hair was as white as fresh, fallen snow, and his hat graced the top of his head like a crown. His face was also tanned darker than normal, and she could tell he had been quite a striking man in his younger days. His mesmerizing, gray-blue eyes twinkled slightly with humor, and radiated kindness as he looked out at the world around him. His face was wrinkled and craggy, and years of laughter had carved gentle wrinkles around his eyes. His hair was just a bit unkept.

"Yes," she said with surprise, "that most certainly is Tillie's father. But he looks much happier than the day we first met him, doesn't he?"

Ophelia agreed.

"It looks like Tillie has brought some happiness back into his life."

"This is interesting. I didn't know he was a church Father. Do you remember him saying anything about that?"

"Nope."

Looking solemn again, Brother Bartholomew spoke up quietly. "It must be done soon or the dragon will leave and take the crown with them."

"Ah, 'tis true," Father Coydon replied softly.

Father Fritz agreed, nodding his head.

"Bob," Father Phillip spoke up, "being who we are, you must take charge, for we cannot enter the mountain. It is all up to you, Henry, and your friends, I believe."

Bob nodded.

Lily wondered who Henry was, but said nothing.

"I do believe we have company, my friends," Father Coydon said, turning slightly and looked off into the forest in the girl's direction. Lily and Ophelia's blood froze.

"Ah, so we do," Father Fritz replied as he and the rest of those around the fire turned and looked into the forest. "Come along, Henry, come stand with us and enjoy the fire."

Otto's big old hound, Henry, ambled slowly closer to the fire where he stopped with a loud rumble in his chest as if he were sighing.

Then, right before their eyes, Henry stood upon his hind legs, gave his body a strong shake and began shapeshifting into an old, grizzled-looking dragon. His long dog snout morphed slowly into the longer-stubbed nose of a dragon as his front paws shortened and attached to large, wrinkled wings. His furry body slowly grew dark blue scales, while long, white whiskers grew from his snout like long nose hairs. Upon his head were two lengthy, white, furry ears, drooping down alongside his face as if they were too tired to stand straight up above his head. Wispy-white whiskers hung from his lower jaw like those of an old man. His enormous eyes were the color of green summer moss; his white, bushy eyebrows were so thick they seemed to block his vision.

With what sounded like a great effort, he lifted his huge wings high above his head, sighed loudly, then plopped down upon his back hunches, flopped forward onto his punchy stomach, and breathed out a couple puffs of smoke then instantly began snoring so intensely that his nostrils were flapping.

"Well, Bob, doesn't look like much help will come from Henry," Father Coydon said, laughing.

"He'll be fine," Bob said, also laughing.

"Wake-up, Hen," Brother Phillip said as he gently tugged on Henry's whiskers. "We have work to do."

Henry opened his eyes, moaned, and rose upon his back legs.

"Ok," Henry mumbled in a deep voice which was exactly what Lily would imagine Henry sounding like if he could speak.

Lily and Ophelia snickered softly as they backed a little further away from the group and quietly moved behind a tall, thick tree. Out of earshot, the two girls stopped, still peering through the tree branches at the group around the fire.

"Did you know Henry was a shape-shifter?" Ophelia whispered.

"No," Lily said, shaking her head. "I've never seen him do that before."

A hush fell across the forest, and the fire slowly began to fade. The girls were instantly aware that the night creatures around them had all become deathly silent. Suddenly they were afraid to even breathe. It was so terribly quiet Lily was sure she would have heard the movement of a ghost if it were possible.

Abruptly those gathered around the fire turned their heads and peered intensely into the forest to their right. Bob and Father Fritz slowly eased closer to the others. In the flicker of an eye, Henry morphed back into an old hound. Suddenly, out from the thick forest flew the apparitions of four horsemen, each riding a great black stallion with glowing red eyes. They were the biggest horses Lily had ever seen. The riders were pushing their horses at a full gallop. What scared the girls even more was; the black-clad riders also seemed to be afraid. Were they running away from something?

Each rider was dressed in black from the top of their head to the soles of their feet; even their faces were covered in black. The feeling of the presence of evil streamed behind them like a thick cloud, but everything was still absolutely silent. Terrifyingly so.

BOOM! The forest glowed orange for a moment as a fifth rider, this one on a tan horse with a white mane, burst into the small clearing on the huge palomino whose hooves were pounding the ground as if on the cobblestone streets of the city. The fifth rider went straight for Bob. Reaching down, the rider swooped Bob up with a colossal arm, tucked him under his armpit like a sack of potatoes, and began to chase the four fleeing riders. Off into the night they flew, leaving behind the echoes of horses' hooves ringing throughout the thick forest.

Frozen in place, the two girls, along with those around the firepit, stood stone-still looking after the five horses and a dangling Bob with open-mouthed astonishment.

Father Fritz, Father Coydon and the two brothers stepped a couple steps back and flopped themselves down on the tree stumps surrounding the firepit. No one said a word for a couple of minutes. Eventually, Henry morphed into the dragon again, lifted his wings and shot into the dark sky like a bullet. He quickly vanished out of sight.

"Well," a voice called out, "if that don't beat all. Have ya ever in your born days seen such a thing? I ain't, that's fur dang sure."

"Good Lord A-mighty, what in the world is going on?" Father Coydon asked as the four of them quickly shifted on their seats, "This forest is full o' critters! Come on out here, whoever ya are!"

Out from the forest emerged not one, but two, hobos. Lily and Ophelia immediately recognized them as Blade and Slick Willy – she had often seen them at the train depot in Caruthersville.

"Where'd you fellas come from? Did you follow those haint's through the forest?" Brother Phillip asked kindly.

"Naw," one replied. "We saw 'em, but we ain't dumb 'nuf to foller 'em! I hear tell that iff'en ya try follerin' haints they'll snatch ya up and take ya up ta' them thur' salt mines up north whur' the winters be so cold yur' fingers fall right off! Ain't wantin' that ta happen!"

"Well, I'm Father Coydon, this is Father Fritz, this is Brother Bartholomew, and this is Brother Phillip." Father Coydon stretched out his hand to shake theirs.

"Well," Blade said, shaking hands with Father Coydon and scratching his matted hair, "seeing that you're church fellas and all, I guess we can tell ya who we are. I'm Blade Lucas, and this here's my brother, Slick Willy. We saw them haints chargin' through the woods like the devil his'self was after 'em, but we din't foller 'em none 'cuz iff'en ya try to citch a haint they turn

184

around and snatch ya right up. Then along came another'n right behind them first ones and he was tearin' up jack to citch 'em."

Slick Willy stood silently beside his brother, nodding his head and shuffling his feet around nervously.

"Ain't that right, Slick?" Blade looked over at this brother.

"Ye – ye - yep, that thur's right," Slick Willy stuttered.

"What are you two fellas doing hiding out in the forest? Are you hungry? Can we get you some water?"

Slick Willy's face lit up like a candle.

"Ye - yep," he stuttered again. "I sure could eat a bite or two. We ain't et' in two days."

"Brother Phillip," Father Fritz said, "get us all something to eat, please. We have plenty to share."

"Thank'ye kindly, Father," Blade said.

"Now," Father Fritz continued as Brother Phillip went to fetch the food for everyone, "please, take a seat and tell me what the two of you were doing in my forest this time of night?"

"*Well*," Blade Lucas said slowly, "we din't know it was *your* forest, so we was jest looking 'round fur some haints and the like. We heard tell thur's a gold crown to be found somer's, too."

Staring at the hobo for a few seconds, Father Fritz spoke slowly.

"Now, don't you think that is a bit far-fetched, fellas?"

"That thur's jest what I been telling 'em, Father," Slick Willy piped up in a squeaky little voice. "But he ain't gonna believe nobody a'tall, iff'en ya know what I mean."

"Well," Blade said, giving his brother's bare foot a sharp stomp, "I'm gonna look fur it anyways. Ain't no harm in tryin' ta find 'hit, is thur, Father?"

"No, ain't no harm in looking," Father Fritz said, shaking his head.

"Well, since yor' a man who knows God purt'-near better anyone else, whur' ya think 'hit might be?"

Father Fritz put his hand on his chin as if in deep thought.

"Hmmm..." he paused. "Well, this is only a guess, mind you, but one would think since all the gold crowns are worn in Europe, it might be hidden in England someplace. What do you other fellas think?"

Father Coydon and the two brothers shook their heads in agreement.

"I'd imagine so. Might be hidden in one of those boneyards where all the long dead kings and queens are buried – the ones that have witches and haints floating around," Father Coydon whispered softly, in an intentionally eerie voice.

Slick Willy shivered and rubbed his arms. Blade swallowed loudly.

"Ya think that really be true, Father?" Blade asked.

"I've seen those ancient tombs of knights and the like. In fact, I've seen witches amongst those big tombstones. Have either of you ever seen a witch spirit?"

"No," Slick-Willy and Blade answered together as they shook their heads, "we ain't never seen that."

"I indeed have," Father Fritz replied with an eerie voice with his eyes bugged out purposely. "I've been close enough to almost touch one, but I knew if I did it would be the last of me."

Brothers Bartholomew and Phillip were also leaning forward staring at Father Fritz with curious eyes. Father Coydon sat on his tree stump with an almost indiscernible grin.

"Well," Father Fritz began his story in a whispery voice as he darted his eyes around the forest so as to give the two Lucas brothers a bit of a scare, "it was a long time ago, so I hope I can remember all the details. It happened in England way before I became a priest. At that time, I was as poor as a church-mouse beggar living on the cold, dark, lonely streets of London, begging for handouts and sleeping in doorways or abandoned stores. A fellow beggar by the name of Chadwick Staunchy told me of Highgate Cemetery where there were places to sleep and not be bothered by the Bobby's with their nightsticks who would occasionally come along and give us a knock on the noggins in the wee hours of the mornings. He said there was a tombstone shaped just like a bed with a marble form of a beautiful woman all snuggled up under a marble blanket. So, I figured I could lay down by that marble lady with my flimsy old blanket and nary a Bobby would bother me since they didn't patrol Highgate. So off I went to Highgate Cemetery to have a look-see for myself. Chadwick said he was not going because he had once been there and the witches chased him off so he was not about to take another crack at it.

"It took me a few hours to make the journey out to Highgate since I had no pounds to take the trolley, but I arrived at the gates to the old cemetery at dusk when the daylight lingers a wee bit in the west, casting its strange, eerie shadows across the ancient headstones. It was quiet as a tomb."

Father Fritz chuckled at his own joke.

"Within minutes, darkness overtook the cemetery as I lingered outside the gate, too nervous to adventure further.

Then, I got up my courage and talked myself into easing through the rusty gates. I could clearly see all the headstones, small and large; many were toppled over.

"Goosebumps jumped upon my arms and shivers tap-danced along my spine. The eyes of unknown beings were upon me and I knew, deep within my soul, those eyes did not belong to a living, breathing human. I knew I was the only flesh and blood being walking the path of that old cemetery. Slowly I walked down the narrow pathway among the graves, pushing the many ground ferns out of my way with my feet and looking closely at each name engraved on the ancient headstones. On the right side of the path were the massive monument headstones of knights, lords and ladies; on the other were the small, insignificant markers of paupers and vagrants whose forgotten lives had faded into the bygone days of long ago; never to be known by modern man. Finally, I came upon the children's' garden plot and immediately, as I put one foot through the little gate separating it from the rest of the graves, something touched the side of my leg. As I looked down, I saw the marble statue of a small girl-child holding a tiny dragon in one arm and touching my leg with the other! The engraving on her tombstone read *Alice Ann Spencer; March 21, 1372 AD – Date of Death unknown.* Well, as I stood frozen in place with that little marble hand against my leg, chills surged through my entire body as if I had been touched by a ghost. I looked into the upturned face of that little statue and I swear its eyes were looking right up at me. They even took on a color. They were as blue as the summer sky and watery as if on the brink of crying when suddenly the moonlight vanished, and the entire cemetery was plunged into a darkness as black as coal. Hushed silence gripped the night air with an icy stillness, and I was sure I could hear my own heart hammering against my chest.

Off to the left, out of the corner of my eyes, I caught a shadow move from one tree to another. From around the back of the tree, slowly there appeared part of a black-hooded being with glowing eyes staring back at me; in a split second, a sharp gust of wind swooped down and swept the being into the night, leaving the moonlight to fill the cemetery once again. With fear within my chest and my skin seeming to crawl, I hunkered down and turned towards the larger tombstones where I could find a place to lay down for the night. Scrambling through the graves I came upon a tomb built above ground with a marble image of someone's dog stretched out as if asleep on top of its master's tomb. Silently I climbed upon the tomb and curled into a ball beside the cold marble dog. It was a large dog with massive, flowing hair so I was able to conceal most of myself beside its stone body. Off to the right was an open field full of low-growing ferns and a few trees. A gentle, warm breeze kicked up and lulled me to sleep, until around midnight or so when the sounds of mumbling woke me from a deep slumber.

"There around a large fire in the open field stood a circle of witches swaying from side to side as if in a trance. All were dressed in black with pointed, hooded capes; those facing me held the glowing eyes of the creature I had spied while in the children's garden.

"The witches stopped doing their moaning and began talking amongst themselves and I could clearly hear what they were saying. They were talking of the little Alice Ann Spencer. One witch, who seemed to be in charge, stated that they must keep anyone from finding her until they had the crown in their possession so as to keep their secret safe for all eternity and another called out that they must continue destroying all who came to hunt for the child and then the entire group nodded their heads in agreement as they muttered their approval. Then, just like that, an icy-cold wind swept down upon us."

Father Fritz stopped speaking as if thinking about his adventure.

"Then what happened?" Slick-Willy faintly whispered. His Adam's-apple bobbed up and down as he sat listening; Blade's mouth hung wide-open. Father Fritz hesitated a bit before continuing.

"Well, there I lay hidden within that icy-cold dog statue, shivering and shaking and thinking I really needed to find a warmer place to sleep, when suddenly I felt that dog move! Its hair started blowing in the cold air and instantly it wrapped it warm body around me like a snug blanket of fur. I could hear that dog rumble deep within its chest and it began licking my head! What a shock it was! I couldn't believe it. I knew there were ghosts and the like running around in this world but never in my born days did I see a marble statue turn into a living creature.

"I wasn't about to complain or move, so I just peeked through the thick, blowing dog hair and watched as the circle of witches scattered and tumbled head over heels into the air where they vanished in the night sky. I don't think they flew. I think the cold wind sweep them up and away into the night. Eventually I fell asleep to the sound of the dog's breathing, but in the morning when I awoke the sun was warm and shining down upon me and the dog had turned back into marble.

"And that my friends," Father Fritz stated firmly, "is when I saw the witches, and why I think, just maybe, the crown you seek is in England, or maybe France. Some of those witches were dressed as French witches. You do know each country's witches dress differently from each other, don't ya?"

Blade and Slick-Willy looked at each other.

"No, we din't know that. We ain't got no money to go over to Europe," Blade said sadly.

"No, we ain't."

"Well, thank-ye Father," Blade stammered. "We ain't going to Europe, so maybe we'll jest try and find some kinda gold here."

"Maybe we can rob something and get the money to go to Europe, Blade," Slick-Willy spoke up happily.

"No," Father Fritz said firmly, "if you do that, I will put a heavenly touch on you and your conscience will make you give it back."

Slick-Willy and Blade looked at Father Fritz, then glanced over and looked at Father Coydon, who was nodding his head in agreement.

"Alright," they both said in unison.

"Come on, Slicky," Blade said as he grabbed his brother's arm and stood up, "let's get out of here and make for Nor' Leans where I know'd whur' some rich folks be laid out."

Stopping sudden-like, he glanced at Father Fritz.

"Whur' some rich folks be livin' and maybe they'll *give* us some money to go on over ta' Europe, I mean," he said awkwardly.

"Good thinking, Mr. Blade," Father Fritz chortled. "Good thinking. When you get there, remember, I will find out if you do any stealing!"

Blade Lucas shuffled his feet around a bit, grabbed ahold of Slick, and took off through the forest in the directions of the river, gabbing and laughing until they were out of earshot.

"Come on, Ophelia," Lily whispered, "let's get out of here." Turning back towards the dirt road, the two of them ran as quietly as possible for the old mansion.

Father Fritz and the brothers began chuckling as Father Coydon laughed right out loud.

"I do believe they will be doing some graverobbing. What do you fellas think?"

Father Fritz nodded, laughing. "I do believe so."

"What are we gonna do about Bob and Henry?" Father Coydon asked.

Father Fritz sat silently for a moment, his elbow on his knee.

"Let's wait and see what the two young gals who were hiding in the forest do.

12

The Gypsy Frog Curse

The road along the Mississippi was eerily quiet and still as Lily and Ophelia walked in silence toward the house on Oak Street. The usual night creatures and insects were silent. A tingling in the air swept along the lane brushing slightly against Lily's arms, causing the hair on her arms to stand on end. Instantly stopping, she slowly put her hand on Ophelia's arm and pulled her into the trees along the dirt road. Once again, they stood behind the trunk of a large elm tree and peered around its thick body looking back at the dusty, narrow road. Slowly and quietly, Lily pulled her black sweater up around her hair and face. She motioned to Ophelia to do the same, since Ophelia's hair was so white it almost glowed in the night.

"We have to find Bob, Ophelia," Lily whispered. "We can't just let him disappear and do nothing. But something is coming along the road."

Visibly gulping, Ophelia nodded; she too felt the change in the night air. Pulling their sweaters over their heads, the two of them stood stone-still watching. Fog began swirling up from the river in small eddies, filling the entire road with a slow-moving, misty haze. It slipped its fingers into the tree line where Lily and Ophelia were standing.

Clip, clap, clip, clap, clip, clap.

The girls heard the sound of running footsteps coming from the direction of the old mansion. Within seconds, out of the mist appeared Blake and Slick Willy.

"Ya see 'er, Blade? Did ya see 'er?" Slick gasped out of breath to his brother in a frightened, stammering whisper.

"Yeah, I see'd 'er. It was pretty quick but I caught a fair-ta-meddlin' good look-see," Blade whispered back, as he too gasped for air.

"Was hit' that old, Miss Josephine?"

"I reckin' hit was."

Blade shook his head in disbelief. He put his hands on his knees and bent down to catch a breath. "Well, it was part her, and part bull frog, iff'en ya can believe that!"

"Oh, I believe ya, I see'd the bull-frog part! Hit was the woman part I couldn't figger out fur a bit."

"I ain't never seen nothin' like it in all my born days! Hit was a frog, I tell ya, a big ol' green, slimy frog! Ol' Josephine's done been cursed inta a frog!"

"Wonder who did it to 'er?" Slicky-Willy whispered, seeming to catch his breath.

"Prolly' that old, red-dressed gypsy woman," Blade said. He glanced around to make sure no one was listening. "She's got some powers I ain't never heard of. I hear tell she turned a whole gang of outlaws inta frogs!"

Slick-Willy grabbed ahold of Blade's arm and shushed him.

The fog began swirling higher and higher until it covered both men from their feet to their waist and began slipping further into the forest where Lily and Ophelia were hiding.

"Hear that?" Slick said quietly, ignoring the swirling fog.

Blade cocked his head to one side as if to get a better listen through the foggy blackness of the night.

"Hit's her as sure as I'm a'standin' here. You hear that bull-frog croak?"

Slick-Willy leaned his long neck out and gave a good listen.

"Yep, I hear'd hit'.

"We best be getting' outta here. Come own," Blade said, tugging on Slick Willy's shirt. "Let's go on out to Dragon Mountain and see iff'en we can find out what's goin' own. Bobby Joe Sikeston said that big ol' dragon with the gold crown is gonna die for sure."

"Well," Slick replied, looking at Blade curiously, "I cain't understand how a haint can die when hit's already dead, but I'll go 'long with ya jest to make sure ya ain't foolin' me none."

Off the two men went running until all Lily and Ophelia could see were the tops of their heads bobbing up and down through the swirling fog.

CROAK, CROAK.

RIB-BIT, RIB-BIT.

Hehe.

CROAK.

Out from the misty gloom emerged a dark figure with the flapping feet of a huge bull-frog shuffling its webbed feet through the haze. Its head was half human and half frog, but its body was all frog - except it was standing upright on its back legs. Its front legs had human hands with long, black fingernails. It was covered with warts from its head to the bottom of its big, slapping hindfeet. At the nape of its thick frog neck was a tight bun of black hair; its hands and arms were a greenish color with what looked to be slimy water dripping from its bent elbows. The rest of its body was an unnatural yellowish-brown. Its eyes were huge frog eyes, and its shoulders were hunched as if struggling to stand upright. Stuck on the top of its head between two giant warts was wedged a large lily-pad with its white flower hanging over the frog's right eye. By the facial features, Lily knew immediately it was indeed Miss Josephine herself in the form of a frog.

Miss Josephine hopped with her back legs, croaked, and let out a long, loud frog fart. The stench was strong; the little blooming flowers along the road withered instantly. Lily and Ophelia's eyes watered as they held their breath and forced themselves not to gag.

Then, fear squeezed their hearts as Miss Josephine stopped, turned, and began shuffling straight towards them. Her enormous mouth opened wide, and a long frog tongue shot out like a bullet and caught a bird flying above the mist. In a split-second, she slurped it into her drooling mouth and swallowed the whole bird with a loud *GULP*.

Ophelia gagged.

"Shh!", Lily whispered, grabbing Ophelia's arm.

The frog whipped its ugly head up and glared in their direction.

"If that's you, Lily Quinn," it muttered out in a distorted croak, "mark my words, you heathen hillbilly, I'm going to get you yet. The ground has trembled once again and its almost your time." She stood there for a few more seconds staring into the dark forest, before turning and hopping towards the river, croaking as she went.

"It's trembling," she croaked. "It's trembling!"

Lily looked at her friend as she asked quietly.

"Did you feel the earth tremble, Ophelia?"

"No," Ophelia whispered, shaking her head.

"Come on," Lily said quietly, "we have to get to the mountain. Bob is in big trouble. I can feel it in my bones."

Slipping out from the trees, the two of them ran through the thick fog to the old mansion and did not stop until they were at the top of the steps where they turned and looked back towards the rushing river. No sign of Miss Josephine or the Lucas brothers. Silently they slipped through the massive door and crept up to their room to decide what and when they would leave for Dragon's Mountain.

13

Death of the Dragon

Before daybreak crested in the east, the two girls tiptoed down the steps and slipped into the kitchen where Katie Patterson was already up getting ready to prepare breakfast.

"I've fixed the two of you a quick breakfast and packed a small bag with food to take along the way," she said softly without turning to see who had entered the kitchen.

Lily and Ophelia looked at Katie questionably. Katie continued talking without turning around.

"Yesterday the authorities caught Charlie Juarez, and he confessed to the killing of our Annabelle and told them Buster T. Tobin was the one who killed Natty during the battle of Chickamauga. He had dressed as an enemy soldier and killed him thinking that way it would be easier to get to Annabelle and find that foolish gold crown. A policeman just now left the house and said they found Charlie Juarez's body by the edge of the river after he escaped jail last night."

Katie turned and placed a plate before each girl.

"Now," she whispered softly with tear-filled eyes, "please, bring our Bob back home where he belongs. Eat up and don't forget the sack lunch."

She spoke so softly the two of them could barely hear her. She turned back to the large cast-iron stove, placed the skillet on a cold burner and turned back to face them. She hesitated as if she wanted to say more, but instead walked quickly out of the warm, toasty kitchen into the chilly hallway leading to the parlor.

Saying nothing more, Lily and Ophelia wolfed down their breakfast, picked up their bags and took off out the door towards the cemetery.

Bursting through the open cemetery gate, they ran until they reached the vertical path leading up to Dragon's Mountain. Gasping for air, Lily put her hands on her knees to catch her breath before beginning the slow, tedious climb up the narrow path.

Halfway up, Lily stopped, cocked her head to one side trying to make out the strange sound reaching her ears. She looked back and shrieked.

"Hold on to the trees!" she yelled to Ophelia.

Whoosh, whoosh, whoosh.

A blanket like cloud of apparitions blew past them, creating a wind so strong the two of them could scarcely hold onto the tree roots. They were literally swept off their feet, but were able to hold on to the tree roots with their hands. Lily was sure both she and Ophelia would be carried to their death down the side of the path. Ophelia's white braids had come loose, and her hair was streaming in the wind. Lily could barely hear Ophelia's screams because of the deafening noise of the apparitions. Suddenly their bodies slammed back against the path as the cloud of apparitions passed. All was suddenly silent.

"I'm going to vomit," Ophelia muttered.

"No you're not," Lily said, catching her breath.

"I'm going to faint," Ophelia responded, panting.

"No!" Lily yelled as she looked back behind them. "Don't do it Ophelia! Look!"

Pointing back down the path behind them, she said, "There's skeletons coming too!"

The moment Ophelia saw them, she hurriedly started scrambling up the path.

"Go faster, Lily! Go!"

Snatching ahold of the next tree root, Lily frantically grabbed the next, the next and the next root until she was at the edge of the plateau. With what seemed like the last of her strength, she pulled herself up and over the edge, then reached back and grabbed Ophelia's hand, giving it a strong jerk. They both landed hard, panting. Immediately, the two familiar skeletons Nevil Bindi and Archie-bald Crumb flung their bone bodies over the edge, followed by more clinking and clanking skeletons behind them.

Stunned, Lily and Ophelia sat upright and stared at the skeletons.

"Why didn't you just fly up here?" Lily asked as she glared at Archie-bald.

Archie and Nevil looked at each other than their bone mouths flew open and their jawbones jerked up and down as they laughed.

"Skeletons can't fly," Archie-bald hooted as he fell on the ground with peals of laughter.

"Or...can we?" he asked Archie-bald with a frown on his face.

"Don't know." Archie replied.

Then the entire mob of skeletons fell on the ground rolling in laughter, not realizing their bones were falling off.

"Hey!" Nevil Bindi finally exclaimed as he sat straight up, "we're falling apart!" he shouted as his bone jaws jerked up and down again with glee.

There was more laughter and rolling on the ground then all the skeletons sat up, looked around at themselves, laughed again, then dove into the pile of bones and began snatching and grabbing for body bones. Some were snatching bones off other skeletons and others were sitting on the ground crying with their bone mouths wide open.

"Let's go," Lily whispered to Ophelia as she eased away from the frenzy. Jumping up, they raced for the thick forest. Just before they entered the shadowy forest, the thick vines hanging from the trees once again parted for them. They glanced back for a second to take in the sight of the skeleton gang. There were skeletons with four legs, some with no legs at all but three or four arms, and one poor fella had no head - the skeleton next to him had two heads! Most had legs, arms, fingers, and hands sticking out from various bones making them look like a bunch of porcupines.

Lily and Ophelia raced through the opening in the forest and within minutes reached the clearing where the big firepit had been. Turning back to look at the path, they realized the hanging moss had closed behind them. Looking up at the vines hanging along the granite wall of the mountain, they could see other creatures climbing the vines.

Suddenly, large claws snatched both of them up. Up the side of the granite wall they flew; within seconds, the mountain before them began shaking violently, causing those climbing the vines to fall back to the firepit clearing, taking the vines along with them. With a loud cry, the dragon carrying them swooped along the wall, and with little effort using its razor-sharp teeth, clipped away every vine still dangling along the wall. Then up it flew with the two of them still clutched tightly in its claws.

Thud.

Approaching another smaller plateau, the dragon dropped them to the ground and vanished, but not before Lily looked up and identified the dragon as none other than their friend Bijou. Stunned, the two of them stood up, brushed the dirt and twigs off their clothes and looked around. Not a single tree was growing on this plateau, and the air was frigid. Approximately thirty feet in front of them was a large, yawning mouth of a cave leading further into the mountain.

"Come on, Ophelia. Maybe it's warmer inside," Lily whispered.

Without hesitating, Ophelia agreed and took off running for the opening with Lily close behind. Coming to a skidding stop at the mouth of the gaping cavern, the two of them eased inside and immediately felt the warmth of a fire. A few more steps further inside, their eyes adjusted and they could see the cavern was much deeper than expected. Cocking her head to one side, Lily could hear a slight, almost inaudible, rustle coming from the path behind them.

"Quick," Lily whispered, pulling her friend into one of the many dark shadowy crevices. Silently they waited for what seemed like an eternity. The smell of rotting food and body sweat filled the air. In through the opening slid the red-dressed old gypsy who stopped immediately and began shifting her eyes quickly around the cavern, searching and spying for anything she found amiss. Slipping in behind her came a giant of a man with a devious look on his face. Lily could tell he was the cause of the odors. He had the dark swarthy skin-tone and long, midnight-black hair of the Romany gypsies. His clothes were filthy, and chunks food were imbedded in his long beard. Around his neck hung a rotted bird of some kind along with a multiple of gold and silver chains.

"I feel something in the air, Danior," the old gypsy spoke as she continued peering around the cavern walls. "Come quick, we must hurry. The good spirits are against us here. I can feel it in my bones. We must be very careful, my son."

"I am ready for them," Danior said, laughing deeply and smiling cunningly as they hurried on through the cavern. His mouth was full of large, yellow teeth.

Slipping quietly from their hiding place, Lily and Ophelia took off their shoes and cautiously followed the old gypsy and her son through the shadows. The only thing lighting the way was a dim glow coming from further inside the cave. Up ahead, the cavern quickly began narrowing until the passage was only about ten feet high and five feet wide. It got warmer with each minute. After a few minutes, they slipping silently through the narrow opening and entered a vast, echoing room which was as silent as a tomb.

Along the sides of the circular room stood many different creatures. A feeling of anticipation filled the air. Looking around the enormous room, Lily spotted Miss Josephine, the frog, wedged into one of the many crevices; a dozen or so apparitions were floating next to her, coming in and out of visible focus. Along the further wall were numerous skeletons, including Nevil Bindi and Archie-bald Crumb. How they got there before she and Ophelia was a wonder. Higher on the walls, on a small ledge above the skeletons, crouched three Gaggolangs, their heinous faces shifting and transforming as they waited in excited anticipation. To the right of Lily and Ophelia stood Shadrack Jones and Chauncey Jenkins, with many other living humans staring silently forward. There on a wide ledge, well above the rest and sitting atop their jet-black, prancing steeds was the horseman apparitions Lily had seen in Father Fritz's forest. Their ebony robes fluttered in an unfelt wind.

In the middle of the wall directly across from Lilly, on a boulder reaching ten or so feet above the rock floor, stood none other than Mr. Kulicki. He was dressed in a long, white robe trimmed in glistening silver; in his right hand he held a tall, thin staff that reached high above his head. Atop the staff sat a crystal-clear sphere with what looked to be a tiny dragon trapped inside. Behind Mr. Kulicki was another open passageway, the same as was behind Lily and Ophelia. Suddenly, with a fierce, nerve-rattling voice sending fear racing down Lily's spine, Mr. Kulicki bellowed.

"Opheliaaaa, move to your right and stand before the opening."

In stunned silence, Ophelia swallowed her fear with an audible *gulp* and began shuffling her feet to the right.

"Make room, humans, make room for Ophelia to pass. Do not touch her, or you shall be vanquished!"

Ophelia scurried to an opening which Lily had not seen. It was identical to the one Lily stood before.

"Bijou," Mr. Kulicki then thundered in a bone-shaking voice, "come forth."

Out from another opening, directly across from Ophelia, emerged Bijou. No longer was he the timid dragon Lily knew. He was a giant of a dragon with red glowing tips on each scale covering his body. He raised his now massive, red-barbed tail and slammed it down onto the ledge upon which he stood, causing small rocks and dirt to fall from the cave's roof. Then, opening his massive mouth, he spewed forth flames that almost reached the other side of the massive cavern.

"Lily!" Mr. Kulicki barked, "Stay where you are."

Instantly, the three openings behind Lily, Ophelia and Bijou slammed shut. The cave became as dark as midnight and as silent as death itself. Uneasy tension quickly grew thick in the air. From deep within the far reaches of the mountain came a deep ticking sound of an enormous clock, echoing through the black chamber.

BOOM!
BOOM!
BOOM!
Each sound shook the mountain.
BOOM!
BOOM!
BOOM!
Lily covered her ears. The noise was uncomfortably loud.
BOOM!
BOOM!
BOOM!
BOOM!
BOOM!
BOOM!

"That must have been a clock marking midnight," Lily thought to herself. She uncovered her ears. It was still completely silent, and completely dark. Then slowly, she noticed a slight golden light appearing in the middle of the room. The light grew in intensity. After a moment, she saw it. A shimmering, gold crown hovering just above the ground. It stayed silent for another second.

Suddenly, with a roar so loud it shook the walls, the entire mob exploded into action.

The black-clad horsemen apparitions surged their horses off the ledge onto the floor of the cave where they landed with ease. Every skeleton and ghost *clinked*, *clanked* and *swooshed* to the bottom of the cave. All the humans jumped, feet-first, off their ledge and landed with *thuds* on the hard-packed floor - except for Chauncy Jenkins who dove head-first onto the floor. He did not immediately get up off the ground and when he did, he staggered a few wavering steps to the left then to the right then stood in one place slowly swaying back and forth for a bit before giving his head a couple shakes and jumping back into the melee.

Lily stood bug-eyed as she watched Miss Josephine the frog waddle to the edge of the ledge, squat down, and with a loud *CROAK*, took a mighty leap and landed on top of Nevil Bindi's skull, which went rolling across the floor. His jaws immediately started flapping up and down, calling out to his body to come pick him up. It wasn't long before his body found him and reattached to his head.

Only the Gaggolangs remained on their ledge for a few seconds, but it was only a moment until they too could not resist. With mouths drooling green slime and grotesque facial expressions, the three slipped and slid over the rim of their ledge then slithered into the chaotic mob of desperate creatures and slipped their silvery fingers around each creature near them.

Three skeletons were fighting a group of ancient, medieval warriors Lily had not noticed before. Archie and Nevil had a warrior pinned to the floor and were doing their best to separate him from his limbs.

Dragons large and small were attacking the humans, but the humans were holding their own with long swords, hammers, and buckets of water. One knee-high sized dragon began spewing fire from his mouth, but a man drenched him with a large bucket of water, causing him to spit and sputter before attacking the man with his front claws. The man grabbed him by the neck and shoved him to the ground; the dragon fell over in a faint, and the man jumped upon the next dragon.

The air filled with smoke from the dragons and the rancid smell of Gaggolang sweat. Shoes, stockings, hats and skeleton bones were flying everywhere. A massive number of apparitions were battling the black-clad horsemen; the horsemen seemed to be prevailing.

Peering closely at the frenzied mob, Lily thought for sure she could see the old Arch Bishop of Canterbury amongst the fracas. His white wig was cockeyed on his head and his poor, worn-out robe was hanging to one side of his body. Then with a jerk from Shadrack Jones, the poor fella's robe fell right off, and there he stood in his long-johns and socks. His shoes had vanished within seconds of the fight and his staff was probably trampled underfoot. After losing his robe, the old bishop stood still for a second in surprise, but quickly jumped right back into the brawl on top of Chauncy Jenkins, giving him a swift bonk on the noggin. Chauncy went down like a sack of potatoes with the bishop on his back. Nevil Bindi came quickly, dragging the old bishop off Chauncy. However, then he himself jumped upon Chauncy and gave him a swift kick, then took off for another encounter with another creature. A Gaggolangs arm slipped around Chauncy's body and began pulling him out of the shuffle before Shadrack appeared and gave the Gaggolang a sharp stomp, making it retreat in a flash.

During the entire brawl, Miss Josephine hopped and croaked brashly off to one side of the melee, careful not to get in the middle of the fracas, with one exception. She latched onto a passing skeleton's arm, give it a jerk, then hopped quickly away as she gobbled up the boney arm and belched loudly.

The din of clanking, clinking and yells filled the atmosphere with vibrations as the free-for-all continued gaining strength. Creatures of all kinds began falling on the floor in droves. It seemed that some were dying, and some apparitions and skeletons were... fainting? A motionless Gaggolang body lay on the cave floor, pulsating in a bright purple glow with every yell from the brawling survivors.

Lily suddenly noticed an orb of light over by Mr. Kulicki. Slowly, beginning with tiny flickers of light, the sphere atop Mr. Kulicki's staff began giving off a dim, amber glow. It grew in intensity, illuminating his face, then his white robe, and then with a sudden, blinding flash, lit up the entire cave like high noon.

"SILENCE!" Mr. Kulicki boomed.

Instantly the clashing creatures froze. Some had their weapons posed high above their heads. Others had their hands around each other's necks. But none dared move a muscle.

Instantly, the cave once again turned black as midnight. To Lily's surprise, not a murmur or movement could be heard. The whole crowd sat in stupefied silence, waiting to see what would happen.

Drip.

Drip.

Drip.

From far in the distance came the sound of water dripping slowly into a pool. Tension was again thick in the air; Lily found herself clenching her fist tightly. Again, the crystal orb atop Mr.

Kulicki's staff radiated its soft amber glow. The tiny captured dragon began spinning a web of some kind.

"This crown belongs only to the rightful owner," Mr. Kulicki thundered. "I care not from where you come nor who sent you. Only the just owner shall receive the crown."

Angry growls and protests erupted within the cave, seemingly shaking the walls. None had succeeded insomuch as touching the shimmering crown.

"Return to the wall!" Mr. Kulicki roared. As if by magic, every creature on the floor was abruptly flung against the walls from where them came before the fracas had begun.

"The crown belongs to the family of Otto Söderberg, and to him it shall go! You creatures have foolishly believed the tales of eternal life that have been passed down through the eons of time. 'Tis no such thing in this world, therefore you shall perish in this cave along with those of you who cause troubles in whatever world you are now living!"

With that said, Mr. Kulicki reached for the orb on his staff and with a mighty roar coming from deep within his being, hurled the orb into the middle of the cave where it hovered suspended in the air, rotating and radiating light throughout the entire cavern.

"Release the web!" Mr. Kulicki bellowed.

Instantly the orb flew toward Bijou, leaving behind the trails of the web it had been spinning inside the orb. Bijou snatched the orb from the air and flung it towards Lily who, without thinking, caught it behind her back and hurled it to Ophelia. She also caught it behind her back, then flung it on to Mr. Kulicki, who passed it again to Bijou. Thus, the ball passed again from Bijou to Lily, to Ophelia, to Mr. Kulicki, many times, and always behind their backs. As the orb flew around and around the cave, it released its web which clung to the creatures positioned on the ledges.

Then, just as suddenly as it had begun, the orb stopped spinning and flew back to the top of Mr. Kulicki's staff with the tiny dragon still enclosed within.

Tick. Tick. Tick.

Once again, a massive clock ticked off the time as all the creatures waited in silence. Up from the floor of the cave arose the shimmering apparition of Draycon the ice dragon. His icy-blue, transparent body was curled around the lovely spirit of Annabelle Bloome, who was dressed in a long, white flowing gown blowing gently in a breeze. Upon the massive dragon's neck still hung the coveted gold crown, glistening in the light of the orb. Both Draycon and Annabelle lay motionless.

A soft rumble came from the top of the cavern, growing in intensity until the top of the mountain split wide open, revealing the midnight-black sky of the universe. Millions of stars twinkled and sparkled above.

All was silent for what seemed to be eternity. Then suddenly without warning, the sound of breaking glass filled the air as the apparitions of Draycon and Annabelle Bloome began breaking into pieces and gently floating towards the open mountain top.

Mr. Kulicki broke the deathly quiet.

"Now, Bijou" he whispered, just loud enough for Lily to hear.

In less than a second, Bijou flew from his ledge, swooped down and slipped his own neck through the gold chain, holding the crown. He flew to the ledges and snatched up Lily and Ophelia and flew up and out through the opening as did the gently floating pieces of Draycon and Annabelle Bloome.

Just beyond the edge of the opening Bijou stopped and quickly turned, hovering close to its edge. The three of them watched the spirit-pieces of Draycon and Annabelle Bloome float out of the mountain and vanish into the blackness of the universe. Without saying a word, Bijou flew like the wind in the direction of the old cemetery of the mansion on Oak Street, circling lower and lower as if hunting for a particular spot in which to land.

Finally, he descended between two high headstones, and with a soft sigh, placed his massive feet upon the ground and placed the crown on the earth before them then gently and carefully laid down, resting his head on the side of one of the headstones.

Rolling off Bijou's back, Lily and Ophelia stood to their feet. There before them sat Henry - Otto's old hound - looking up at them happily. Stunned, Lily and Ophelia looked back at Bijou. In the light of the midnight moon, the big dragon began to age very quickly. His shimmering green scales slowly turned gray as he sighed deeply.

"I am tired" he whispered softly, "Tis been a long time."

Then his huge body began to morph into that of a human.

Staring with amazement, Lily and Ophelia watched as Bob's body appeared before them, right where Bijou the dragon had stood thirty seconds earlier. Bob's eyes opened, looked at them with a smile then he too vanished into the grave plot upon which he lay.

WOOF!

Henry the hound held the crown in his mouth, and after a slight pause, took off running towards the old mansion faster than an old dog should be able to run. Lily and Ophelia looked at each other, then down at the headstone over which Bob had disappeared. It read:

Robert T "You can call me Bob" Söderberg
Born: Unknown - Died: Unknown

INTERESTING FACTS:

Llywelyn ap Gruffudd's Coronet Crown

Llywelyn, which means Our Last Leader, was Prince of Wales (Latin: Prince Wallie; Welsh: Tywysog Cymru from 1258 until his death at Cilmeri in 1282. The son of Gruffudd ap Llywelyn Fawr and grandson of Llywelyn the Great, he was the last sovereign prince of Wales before its conquest by Edward I of England.

Llywelyn ap Gruffudd, sometimes written as Llywelyn ap Gruffydd, also known as Llywelyn the Last, rarely styled as Llywelyn Yr Ail, was Prince of Wales from 1258 until his death at Cilmeri in 1282.

Born: 1223
Died: December 11, 1282, Aberdeen, United Kingdom
Spouse: Eleanor de Montfort, Princess of Wales (m. 1278)
Royal house: Aberffraw
Children: Gwenllian of Wales
Parents: Gruffudd ap Llywelyn Fawr Senana ferch Carado

The Crown of Llywelyn ap Gruffudd, the coronet of Llywelyn ap Gruffudd, the last king of Wales, was seized along with other holy artifacts at the end of the Conquest of Wales by Edward I, in 1284, and was taken to London, and kept with the crown jewels in Westminster Abbey until they were stolen in 1303. It was not present in the inventory taken during the destruction of the crown jewels by Oliver Cromwell in 1649, and remains unaccounted for (June 1282 – 7 June 1337) was the only child of Llywelyn ap Gruffudd.
Gwenllian of Wales was suspected as being the one who stole back her father's crown.

Made in the USA
Middletown, DE
26 August 2021